CADE'S REVENGE:
THE WESTERN ADVENTURES
OF CADE MCCALL

Also by Robert Vaughan

THE WESTERN ADVENTURES OF CADE MCCALL
Long Road to Abilene
Cade's Redemption

THE FOUNDERS SERIES
Lost Lady of Laramie
The Ranchers
The Raiders
Warriors of the Code
Hearts Divided

THE REMINGTON SERIES
Red River Revenge
Good Day for a Hangin'
Showdown at Comanche Butte

CADE'S REVENGE: THE WESTERN ADVENTURES OF CADE MCCALL

ROBERT VAUGHAN

WOLFPACK PUBLISHING

LAS VEGAS

WOLFPACK
PUBLISHING
— EST 2013 —

Wolfpack Publishing
6032 Wheat Penny Avenue
Las Vegas, NV 89122

ISBN 978-1-62918-586-6

Robert Vaughan

Prologue

Twin Creek Ranch, Howard County, Texas – 1927:

OWEN WISTER STEPPED OFF THE PORCH of the ranch house belonging to Cade McCall. He walked across the lawn that was wet with dew as he made his way to the bunkhouse.

"Good morning, Mr. Wister. We thought you weren't coming this morning," one of the ranch hands said.

"You knew I'd be here," Wister said making his way to the coffeepot that sat on the back of the cook stove.

"Did you forget your cup again?" the cook asked as he pulled a pan of hot biscuits from the oven.

"I did," Wister said as he slapped his forehead. "It was setting right beside my typewriter. I'll go get it."

1

"No, no. We've got plenty," the cook said as he took a cup down from a hook. "I don't know how you remember anything with all those words swirling around in your head."

"This book is easy," Wister said. "Your boss has a lot to say, and all I'm doing is recording his story."

"All of us want to read your book when it's done," one of the roustabouts who was sharing the bunkhouse said. "Leastwise those of us who can read." He threw a towel at one of the young men who was sitting quietly at the end of the table.

"Aw, come on now," the young man said. "I'm trying to learn real good."

A couple of the men laughed. "You can't fool us, Davey. You could read the minute you joined this outfit. It's your teacher you're after."

A broad smile crossed Davey's face. "Well now, you tell me, if you could find a way to spend time with Miss Amanda, wouldn't you do it?"

"I believe you've made your point," Wister said. "Mr. McCall's granddaughter is a charming young woman, and I'd want to find a way to spend time with her, too, if I were one of you."

"We'd all like to do that, but she's partial to the cow men. She don't seem to like to be around the oil men."

"Course not," Davey said. "You oil men stink."

"And cow men don't?" a roustabout asked.

"I think I'd better get back to the house," Wister said as he grabbed a biscuit, then put a slice of fried ham on it. "I don't want to be here when the argument heats up."

"Ah, we're just funnin' with one another," Davey said. "We know the oil men make it possible for Twin Creek Ranch to pay its hands the best of any outfit around here."

"Yeah, it seems every ranch in Howard County's got oil money coming in, but it's the McCalls who take care of their help."

Owen Wister left the bunkhouse and made his way back to the main house. It was a two-story white clapboard house with a red roof and red shutters. He smiled. A chapter in the book he was writing about the life and adventures of Cade McCall came to mind. He hadn't thought about it, but he wondered if the red trim on the house was a way of paying homage to Arabella DuPree and her place of business known as The Red House.

He knew that Arabella, or Chantal as she was known in New Orleans, had played a significant role in Cade's life. It had been she who had caused him to be shanghaied and put on a ship bound for South America, and it had been his quest to find her that brought him to Galveston. And from Galveston, his reconnection with Jeter Willis, a friend who had been with Cade at the Battle of Franklin, got him into the cattle business.

Wister picked up his pace as he passed the wood fence that enclosed the yard of the house. He caught a scent of the roses that rambled over the rails, and he couldn't pass the bright red blooms by. He lifted a cluster to his nose and took in the aroma.

"That's why I fool with those things."

Wister looked toward the porch where he saw an elderly gentleman sitting in a porch swing.

"They're beautiful," Wister said as he continued up to the house.

"Did you get a lot done last night?" Cade asked.

"Yes. Are you ready to go to work?" Wister asked.

Cade McCall chuckled. "Work? All I'm doing is talking. I've never considered that work."

"I think I'm caught up and I'm ready to listen today. Have you thought about what you want to tell me?"

"I'll just start talking and we'll see what comes up," Cade said.

1

The LP Ranch, Jackson County, Texas

CADE MCCALL, JETER WILLIS, and several of the cowboys who had made the spring cattle drive to Abilene, passed under an arch that had a black lettered, white sign welcoming visitors to the premises.

LP RANCH
LINUS PUCKETT OWNER
CATTLE AND HORSES

"Get these horses into the corral and see to it that they get a good helping of oats; then put them out in the canyon pasture. Oh, and one of you had better ride out and make sure the tank has water in it," Cade ordered. "Boo, you check the windmill. Make sure the pump is working."

A big smile crossed Boo Rollins' face as he saluted Cade. "Yes sir, boss man. I'll get right on it, but it's only because I feel a responsibility to these here animals we been a livin'

4

with all these days. Not because you told me to do it, ya understand."

Cade shook his head. "You're right. Technically, we were hired to get the herd to Abilene, and that we did. Now these horses are Mr. Puckett's responsibility."

"I see no reason why you should stop giving orders," a man said as he walked toward them. "You made good time getting the horses back."

"We had good weather," Cade said as he dismounted, offering his hand to Linus Puckett.

"That always helps. About you giving orders, Cade, I'm serious. My foreman had to go back East for who knows how long? Would you consider hiring on for that job, at least until Coley gets back?"

"He can't," Jeter said. "If he's going to be ranchin' he can stay right on the MW with me--course that will never be. He'll be high tailin' it to Galveston as soon as we clear the LP gate."

"I'm not leaving yet," Cade said. "I expect you'll be wanting to hear my report."

"That I do," Puckett said. "I got your telegram a while back and I couldn't be more pleased with what you got for my cows. You're a good man, Cade."

"I couldn't do it by myself. Jeter does just as much as I do, and we had an exceptional crew this time," Cade said.

"Exceptional. I'd say that might be an exaggeration," Jeter said. "If you think Ike Weldon was an exceptional cook, there's something wrong with your head."

"Well, that's true," Cade said, "but we all survived."

Puckett laughed. "That's why Agnes has a treat for you. Come on in. She's got hot crullers coming out of the grease right now."

"That's what I smell," Jeter said as he hurried toward the main house.

"I think you'll be very pleased," Cade said as he removed a satchel from his horse.

"What about Andy Miller? Did you get a chance to check up on him on the way back down?" Puckett asked.

"We didn't see him, but the fellows at Red River Station said they took him to Decatur. They said his spirits are up, but he'll never walk again. He took a nasty fall."

"Too bad. He was a nice kid," Puckett said as he opened the door.

The smell of freshly made pastries filled the house, and even though Cade wasn't particularly hungry, he salivated in anticipation. Jeter was already sitting at the table, a plate filled with crullers in front of him.

"Oh, Cade, you look thin," Agnes Puckett said as she embraced him. "I've got a plate of crullers for you, too, just as soon as I can take them up."

"They certainly smell good, but I think I can only eat a couple," Cade said.

"Pooh," Agnes said. "We'll just see about that."

Cade sat down at the table and opened the satchel withdrawing several neatly-bound stacks of bills that he put on the table. He also took out a ledger book.

"We lost a hundred and thirty-seven cows, but we made up thirty of them with unbranded range cattle. We killed sixteen for meat and we traded off forty along the way--some to grangers for fresh vegetables, meat, eggs and such, and some we gave to Indians. Our biggest single losses were eighteen that were crushed in the mill after a hailstorm, and . . ." Cade stopped for a minute. ". . . and eleven that drowned when Andy was hurt at the Red River." Cade cleared his throat as he continued his report. "There were fewer than a dozen stampedes and the fifty-two remaining cows that were lost were either not recovered or else they just wandered off or died.

"We left here with thirty – three hundred head, and we reached Abilene with three thousand, one hundred and ninety-three. After deducting all expenses, including what Jeter and I will receive, you net $31,586."

"Very good, boys!" Puckett said, rolling his eyes as he quickly calculated the figures in his head. "That comes close to ten dollars a head. Not bad for some cows that not too many months ago were roaming the brush of South Texas. You did a fine job."

"More crullers?" Agnes asked as she exchanged an empty plate for a full one.

"I've not had anything this good since we left Abilene. There's a little restaurant up there that serves the best pies. When we get back, I'll have to talk Mrs. Wagner into adding these to her menu," Jeter said, taking two more of the pastries.

"I'm glad you're planning on making another trip," Linus Puckett said as he began counting out sixty-five hundred dollars apiece for Cade and Jeter. "Can I count on you ramrodding for the LP again next year?"

"Yes, sir," Cade said. "It's a pleasure working for a man like you."

Caldwell, Kansas:

Amon Kilgore was having a drink in the Longhorn Saloon with Sid Gorman.

"Where are they now?" Gorman asked.

They're in a gully, west of town, twelve hundred of them. I can let you have five hundred for twelve dollars a head," Kilgore said.

"Huh, uh, that's too much. I'll give you five dollars."

"Five dollars? Why would I do that? As it is, I'm gettin' four dollars a head for deliverin' 'em, 'n all I have to do is take 'em on up to Abilene."

"What are they paying in Abilene?" Gorman asked.

"Last word I had they was payin' eighteen dollars, right now," Kilgore said.

7

"I won't be able to get that much for them. I'll have to find someone who's willin' to take 'em."

"There's no way you won't find someone who'll give you fifteen dollars."

The two men continued to negotiate, until Gorman agreed to pay ten dollars. After that, Gorman went to the bank and withdrew five thousand dollars.

Amon Kilgore, Sid Gorman, and Leonard Chestnut who worked for Sid, rode out to the herd of cattle that were trailing to Abilene, Kansas. They could hear the cattle before they could smell them, and they could smell them before they saw them. When they did see the herd, it was like a large undulating island on a sea of grass. Seeing the three men approach, Jerry Alcorn rode out to meet them.

Do we have a deal?" Alcorn asked.

"That we do," Kilgore said, "and this here's the man who made it. Jerry this is Sid Gorman and his man."

"And how much is in it for us?"

"Jerry, Jerry . . . you've got to have patience in this game," Kilgore said.

"Well how much?" Alcorn continued. "It's got to be worth my while to cheat old man Dennis."

"Does five hundred dollars sound about right?"

Alcorn nodded his head. "I think all the boys can live with that. How many is our friend gonna take?"

"I agreed to take five hundred off your hands," Gorman said.

"Good, it'll just make our job easier," Alcorn said. "We'll cut 'em out right now. Don't suppose you're too finicky about the brands you'll be gettin'."

"Can't say that I am," Gorman said. "Where these are goin', nobody cares."

While Kilgore and Gorman watched, Chestnut joined Alcorn and several of the other men as they quickly cut out five hundred head of cattle. When they had them separated, Alcorn returned to the two men.

"Now that you've got the critters, what you goin' to do with 'em?" Alcorn asked. "You and Chestnut gonna herd 'em by yourself?"

"He's got a point," Kilgore said. "What are you going to do with 'em?"

"I've got a place staked out no more'n ten miles from here," Gorman said. "I thought you might see to it that I got them there."

"I think with the two of you, it wouldn't take but a couple more to handle five hundred cows," Alcorn said.

"What about it, Amon? Can you let a couple go for a day or two?"

"If you'll pay them fifty dollars apiece."

Gorman hesitated a moment, then he nodded. "Damn, Kilgore, you trying to get every cent you can."

Amon Kilgore smiled. "Hell Sid, it ain't for me. It's for my men."

"Sure it is. I'll bet the damn punchers don't see a penny of this hundred dollars." Gorman took out a wad of paper money and pulled off the necessary payment. "One of these days, you're gonna run up against someone who won't let you take advantage of 'em."

"Keep your money. I'll keep my men."

"No, no. If I can't get these cows to the holding pen, I've lost them."

"That's how I thought you'd see it."

Kilgore turned his horse and trotted off toward the remaining herd that now numbered close to eight hundred. He had started out with fourteen hundred cows, and up to this point, he had lost fewer than a hundred head. He had to admit he had done a good job acting as the trail boss for the Rocking D and a part of him felt some remorse. But then he thought of the one thousand dollars that he now had in his pocket. By sharing the money with the crew, and he thought he was being extra generous, not a single one of them would ever report back to John Dennis just how they lost so many cows. He could hear their stories now: Indian raids, stampedes, hailstorms, river crossings, and rustlers.

He chuckled. Nobody would mention that 'they' were the rustlers.

"Come on Barney," Cade McCall said as he coaxed his horse off the train at the Galveston, Houston and Henderson depot. "We're almost home. You'll have a dry stable tonight, and I'll have a comfortable bed."

He saddled the horse quickly but didn't bother to mount, deciding instead to lead him through the streets of Galveston. Even though he had been gone for less than four months, the city had changed, and everywhere he looked he saw construction. There were more and more businesses opening, and bigger and bigger houses, all built to accommodate the new millionaires. Galveston had become the main port for the export of Texas products, the principal one being cotton. Most anything that was needed on the Texas mainland was imported through here, and money was flowing causing many to nickname the city the Wall Street of the South.

He smiled when he saw what he was looking for, and he hurried toward an establishment called The Red House. He was half owner of this boarding house, but it was not his half of the business that enticed him to return to Galveston--it was the owner of the other half that drew him.

His partner was Arabella Dupree, a beautiful Cajun from New Orleans, to whom French came easier than English. She spoke with an accent that Cade found most appealing.

Their relationship had a most inauspicious beginning. Cade had met Arabella at a bar in New Orleans. She was using the name Chantal at the time. Arabella had set him up to be shanghaied. And though she hadn't set out to steal from him, he had left behind almost fifteen hundred dollars, which she saw fit to appropriate. For any reasonable thinking man, he should hate this woman--but that was definitely not the feeling he had for her now, and he couldn't wait to see her.

"Well if it isn't the rooster come home to take over the henhouse," a man called when Cade got to the boarding house.

"Mr. Bowman, you know that's not true," Cade said as he tied his horse to the hitching post. "It's Arabella who rules this roost."

"That she does," Bowman said, "and just you wait 'til you meet the new person she's brought in."

"A new resident? Has he taken over my room?"

"Not a he."

"Then it's a woman. That's good," Cade said. "There are too many men living in this house. Mrs. Rittenhouse and Miss Baker must be happy."

"We all like her--we like her a whole lot, but she kinda . . . ."

"Kinda what?"

"She tells us what to do, even more than Miss Arabella does." Mr. Bowman picked up a paint brush. "You see this here brush? Miss Magnolia says you can't call this place The Red House unless we have more red. I'm supposed to paint the porch railings to match the shutters and the roof. Why she even thinks I should paint a rocking chair or two."

"Miss Magnolia is it? Well, it will be interesting to meet her."

When Cade went into the house, he saw Arabella sitting at the piano, and it was positioned in a bay window in a way that made her unaware of his entrance. She was playing a piece by Chopin, and because she was obviously lost in the music, Cade didn't interrupt her. He waited until the last chord resonated, then he applauded, softly.

Arabella turned, and seeing Cade she jumped from the piano bench and rushed to him.

"You're back," she said throwing her arms around him.

"I take it you missed me," Cade said as he kissed her. She was a very attractive, petite young woman with dark hair and flashing black eyes.

"Oh I did," Arabella said. "But now you are back." Her eyes opened wide. "Or will you have to go again?"

"Not this year. I'm here to take over the chicken coop."

Arabella contorted her face. "I do not know what you mean—this *poulailler*, chicken coop," she translated quickly.

"It's nothing. Just something old man Bowman said. By the way, he says we have a new tenant."

"Not exactly. She's a new employee."

"Oh?" Cade said, "And she lives here?"

"She does. Come, let me introduce her."

Arabella led Cade to the kitchen where an attractive young woman was standing at the stove, stirring a pot. She was taller than Arabella, and her coloring was a bit darker, but she was quite attractive in an exotic sort of way.

"Magnolia Trudeau, meet Cade McCall."

"If what I'm smelling is thanks to you, I'm happy to meet you, Maggie."

"It's Magnolia," Arabella insisted, hitting Cade on the arm. "I believe you may have met her once before, but you didn't know her name."

"Oh?" Cade said as he raised his eyebrows.

"I worked with Arabella at Lafitte's Blacksmith Shop Bar in New Orleans," Magnolia said. "When I had a customer that . . . ."

"You don't have to say anything more," Cade said, holding up his hand to stop her. "I know Arabella is happy to have an old friend join her here in Galveston."

"Thank you, Mr. McCall."

"No, no. It's Cade." He stepped to the stove and looked down into the pot. "What is this concoction you've put together?"

"It's *coq au vin*," Magnolia said. "I hope you like it."

2

Rocking D Ranch, Matagorda County, Texas:

Amon Kilgore was reporting to John Dennis, owner of the Rocking D Ranch. Like Cade McCall, Kilgore was a contractor who took herds north.

"I'm sorry to say that we reached Abilene with only seven hunnert 'n ten cows," Kilgore said.

"Seven hundred and ten cows out of fourteen hundred?" Dennis said. "That's one hell of loss!"

"Yes, sir, but it was a real rough drive. We lost three hunnert 'n seventeen to rustlers. 'N we lost another hunnert 'n forty one drownded in the Brazos, the river bein' high 'n all. We had two bad stampedes, 'n in the first one we lost eighty-seven cows, 'n and the second, we lost forty-two. The rest of 'em was cows that just died on the trail from thirst, or one thing 'n another. 'N then the injuns up in The Nations, why, them sorry bastards would sneak in at night 'n take ten or twenty head without nobody even noticin' it. Hell, I didn't know we was that far down 'till it come time to sell 'em to a broker. We got twelve dollars apiece for the seven hunnert 'n ten head we had left."

"Twelve dollars a head? Linus Puckett got fifteen dollars a head for his cattle."

"Yes, sir, that's on account of he got his herd there first. By the time we got there, truth is, they was pretty full up 'n wasn't hardly buyin' no more. After expenses, 'n my charge, you come up with $4,140."

Dennis shook his head. "Four thousand dollars for a year of payin' wages 'n tendin' to the cattle? That's damn little for a year's operation," he said.

"Yes, sir, well, seein' as I only get paid for them cows that I actually deliver for you, well, truth is, I didn't make out none too well myself neither," Kilgore said, as he slid the money across the table to the rancher. He smiled. "But, if we get us a good, early start next year so's that we're near 'bout the first ones to get there, we'll get a real good price for 'em, I know we will."

"Assuming we get enough cattle through," Dennis replied.

"You can't go blamin' none of that on me," Kilgore said. "You been in the business long enough to know that sometimes things like that happens. Hell, I've known ranchers that, some years, winds up actual losin' money."

Dennis ran his hand through his hair, and let out a long sigh in disappointment. "That's true," he said. "I suppose, under the circumstances, I should take some comfort in the fact that I didn't actually lose any money. Thank you, Mr. Kilgore."

"We'll do better next year," Kilgore said with a reassuring smile.

As Kilgore rode away from the ranch, the smile on his face grew broader. Even after paying off the men, he had wound up with more money than the owner. And the drovers, whom he had personally selected, wound up with four times as much money as any other drover made during

14

the entire season. It was that increase in their pay that bought, not only their compliance in his rustling scheme, but also their silence.

Galveston, Texas:

It was getting on into late September, and during the time since Cade had returned from the cattle drive, he had invested much of his share of the income into expanding The Red House. He was building an additional wing that would allow them to double the number of residents they could accommodate. Of course, that meant enlarging the kitchen, and the dining room as well.

He also owned 40% interest in the Bell and Sail, a ship's chandler near the Galveston docks. His interest in the business was economic only; he took no part in managing it, though he did visit the place frequently. He had a connection to the business because Cade had been a sailor at one time. He wasn't a sailor by choice, he had been shanghaied at a bar in New Orleans, and wound up on board a ship that was bound for San Francisco, by way of the horn. Jumping ship in Argentina, Cade made his way back to the States.

As Cade stood on the dock, he noticed that the sea was rolling in, in long, flat, swells, indicative, he had learned, of a storm far out in the Gulf. He saw a ship, sail up, over the distant horizon. He watched the ship until it was hull up, then he stepped back into the Bell and Sail.

"Stan, you got 'ny idea what ship that might be, coming in?"

"It's probably the *Success,*" Stan Virden replied. "It's supposed to make port here, today."

"The *Success?* Hmm, I've got a friend on the *Success.* I wonder how long she'll be in port?"

"I think she'll be here at least a week."

"Good." Cade walked back to the window and looked out over the Gulf again. "Have you seen the water? The long swells like that? That doesn't look good."

"Oh, I expect it'll be nothin' more 'n a few hours of blow 'n some rain," Virden replied.

Cade left the Bell and Sail, then stepped over to the Island Lumber Company to buy some more building material for the expansion of The Red House. After arranging for a livery, he returned to the dock where he saw the *Success*, sails now riffed, being towed in by a screw powered tug boat. He stood on the dock and waited as the ship was brought into its berth, watching the sailors bustling about on deck, getting ready to drop anchor.

"Linemen, fore 'n aft!" someone shouted, and Cade smiled, because he recognized Josiah Burke. Cade had sailed with him on board the *Fremad*. "Pops" as he had been called was then one of the able bodied. On board the *Success*, he was an officer.

When the ship lay along dock secured by large hawsers, fore 'n aft, shore leave was granted. With a yell, the watch, which drew the first shore leave, came hurrying down the gang plank. Burke was the last one down, and seeing Cade he smiled, and came toward him.

"I was hopin' I'd get a chance to see you while we were in port."

"It's damned good to see you, Pops, or can I still call you that now that you're an officer?" Cade asked as the two shook hands.

"That depends. Is there a drink in it for me?"

"You can count on it. Come on. I'll buy."

"Of course you will," Pops said. "A boarding house and a ship's chandler. Next time I come you'll be ownin' a cotton factor."

Although there were many saloons in Galveston, the two that Cade visited most often were the Saddle and Stirrup, and the Anchor Saloon. The Anchor was frequented by seamen, both those to whom Galveston was their home port, and those to whom Galveston was but a port of call.

"So, tell me lad, when will ye be goin' to sea again?" Pops asked, as he took a drink of his grog.

"When the sun rises in the West and sets in the East," Cade said resolutely.

"Aye, well, your time at sea wasn't a good experience for you, I'll grant ye that. But, if you're servin' with a good captain and fair officers, 'n if you're sailin' with a good crew, there's no better place to be in the world than on the deck with the spray in your face, the taste o' salt water on your lips, 'n the sweet soundin' whisper of the wind in full sails."

Cade laughed. "I swear, Pops, you can almost make it sound good, but you forgot to mention being tossed about in heavy seas, baking under a scorching sun, or sailing with cruel officers."

"But I'm a first mate now, 'n you know I'd be fair."

"Too bad you weren't first mate when we were on the *Fremad* together," Cade said.

"I know your experience at sea wasn't all that good, but I'd be willin' to wager that the cow business has its own problems."

"Oh, you mean hostile Indians, rustlers, going days without water, sick cows, stampedes, lawless cow towns, and hands that wander off?" Cade replied. "Well, yeah, there is that, I mean, if you want to dwell on it."

"'Tis not the *Fremad*, I'm speakin' of," Pops said. "'Tis the *Success*, and I'm sure you know that it belongs to Tait Shipping Line."

"I know. Have you seen young Willoughby?"

"That I have. 'Twas none other than he, hisself, who put me on the *Success* as first mate."

Willoughby Tait had been shanghaied along with Cade, and was aboard the *Fremad*. The ironic twist was that Willoughby's family was the owner of a large competing shipping line that sailed out of Boston. It had been the inhumane treatment of Tait that had caused Cade to kill a man while on board ship. With Pops' help, Cade and Bento Hernandez, another of the shanghaied crew, had jumped ship near Buenos Aires and made their way back to the United States.

"How's the boy doing?" Cade asked.

"He's as fine a man as you'd ever want workin' in the office of the company you're sailin' for," Pops said.

"Good, I'm glad for him, and for you, for getting such a good position. If for some reason I did have to go back to sea I could think of no better berth than to be on the *Success* with you as first mate."

"So, tell me, Lad, are you buttoned down for the storm?"

"What storm?"

"Did you learn nothin' while sailin' before the mast? Can you not read the sea, lad?"

"I've noticed it," Cade said. "Looks like there's a storm out there, somewhere."

"More than just a storm, 'tis a hurricane that's comin'," Pops replied. "It's goin' to be a big one, 'n I expect there'll be damage done. I've seen 'em like this before."

"What makes you think it'll be a hurricane, rather than just a storm?

"Have you checked the barometer lately?"

Cade laughed. "I can't say that's something I do every day."

"I checked it before I left the ship. It's at 28.8, 'n fallin'. Why, droppin' like it is, I wouldn't doubt but that it'll get below 28 before all is said 'n done. 'N it won't take it long to get there, neither. I can feel it in my bones, Cade m' boy, 'n I ain't never wrong. Oh, I'm wrong 'bout some things, I'll 'fess up to that quick enough. But when it comes to the storms, I ain't never wrong."

* * *

After he left The Anchor Saloon, Cade took a walk down to the beach where he saw a ribbon of clouds hanging out over the Gulf of Mexico. The clouds looked heavy with rain, but there was nothing threatening about them. The swells he had seen earlier had now become a heavy surf with high waves breaking on the beach, and sending the spindrift flying.

The strange thing though, as far as Cade was concerned, was the wind. It was coming from the north, which would normally mean there would be little to no surf, and yet, here it was.

What neither Cade nor most of the other residents of Galveston knew was that for the last three days, Western Union had been sending telegraphic messages to all its stations along the Gulf Coast saying a storm had passed through the Straits of Florida. They could not predict where the storm would be heading, but they wanted their offices to be prepared.

The clouds, and the surf, were the leading edge, and the mayor had ordered that storm flags fly, but that signal went unheeded. Everyone was aware of the flags, but few residents understood the significance of them.

Cade lingered on the beach watching the clouds and the surf, and wondering if Pops was right about an impending storm. At second glance, the clouds did appear to be more ominous, blacker, and with embedded lightning flashes.

He had never been through a hurricane, though when he was a boy back in Tennessee he had experienced tornados. He had been through heavy storms at sea, and he had endured strong thunderstorms and hail while driving a herd of cattle from Texas to the shipping point in Kansas. But this would be his first experience with a hurricane, if indeed it turned out to be a one.

Cade left the beach and walked along the Strand. For the most part all the activity that characterized this most interesting street was still carrying on as usual. The drummer who called himself the King of Pain was hawking his patent medicines from his wagon as the hurdy-gurdy man dispatched his trained monkey to beg for coins. No one seemed to be alarmed except as he passed Monsieur Alphonse's restaurant, he noticed a man closing all the shutters.

He wondered if something should be done to prepare The Red House. Arabella had been raised in New Orleans and she would be familiar with hurricanes, but when he had left the house, she did not seem concerned. He wished his partner, Jeter Willis, was here. He had grown up in Galveston and he would know what to do. But when the cattle drive season was over, Cade spent the time in town, while Jeter lived out at the MW, the small ranch in Jackson County that the two owned together.

As he approached the house, he saw the delivery wagon from the Island Lumber Company standing at the end of the walkway.

"You know who ordered this?" the driver asked.

A man who was sitting in a rocking chair on the wide porch stood up.

"No, sir, I don't, but I expect the one coming this way knows."

"Is that so, mister," the driver said. "Where do you want this here lumber?"

By now Cade felt a quickening of the wind, and intuitively he felt it would not be good to have loose lumber laying around if the wind got any stronger.

"I'm not sure I want it just yet," Cade said. "Could you deliver it tomorrow?"

"I expect I could," the driver said, "but you'll have to pay me to take it back."

Cade laughed. "How much?"

"Maybe a quarter."

Cade withdrew a quarter from his pocket and gave it to the man.

"You shouldn't have done that, Cade," David Andrews said. "You'll never see your lumber again."

"Well, I'm glad you saw the transaction if I have to prove what I did," Cade said. "The lumber company would never dispute the word of an attorney."

"An old attorney," Lee Bowman said. "He can't even remember what day it is, so you better not depend on him." He was studying a checkerboard as he sat across a table from another resident.

"Then I'll have you as my witness," Cade said. "You know Mr. Bowman cheats, don't you, Mr. Cline?" Cade came up the steps and looked over the game.

"Of course I cheat," Lee Bowman replied with a wave of his hand, though he didn't look away from the checkerboard. "How else can I beat this conniving bastard?"

Cade and David Andrews laughed, but Mr. Bowman and Mr. Cline did not react to the comment.

"We goin' to get some rain?" David asked as he looked toward the sky.

"Sure looks like it," Cade said.

"Good, we could use a little."

"That's true, but a friend of mine who just came in on the *Success* thinks we may be in for a blow."

"You mean a storm?"

"Could be. He says I might be in for my first hurricane." Cade said as he stepped inside.

"A hurricane? Who says that?" Arabella asked, when she heard Cade's comment.

"An old friend I ran into at the Anchor."

"And who was that?"

"Someone you introduced me to."

"You met someone who I introduced to you?"

"I've told you about Pops--Josiah Burke. We were on the *Fremad* together."

"Oh, uh, yes," Arabella replied, as she dropped her head.

21

Cade recognized Arabella's contrition. "I didn't mean anything. It was good seeing an old friend again." Cade lifted her chin. "And I told you, the past is the past."

"I don't know what I've done to deserve you," Arabella said.

"It's your pretty smile," Cade replied, as he kissed her gently.

"Magnolia is making veal cordon bleu for dinner," Arabella said as she moved away from him. "I think you'll enjoy it."

Cade chuckled. "Yes, I could force myself to eat it."

3

At that moment, Cade happened to glance through the window, and when he did, he saw that the limbs of the live oak were waving and twisting rather dramatically. He went back out into the common room where he saw that the boarders who had been out on the porch, had come inside.

"Getting worse?" Cade asked of no one in particular.

"I'd say," Gene Cline replied. "The wind's kickin' up a mite."

"How about a couple of you helping me get in the rocking chairs?"

"You might close the shutters too," Arabella suggested.

Elmer Beck, a seaman who made The Red House his home when his ship was in port, joined Cade and David Andrews.

Andy French, one of the younger residents, and Gene Cline went with Cade and began to close the Bahama shutters.

When they stepped out onto the porch the wind was blowing so strong now that the chairs were rocking back and forth violently. Two had been blown into the railing causing spindles to break. The rain had started as well, and it seemed to blow sideways as it hit Cade's face, stinging him like little needles. To Cade's surprise, Q Street, which such a short time before had been dry, was now a flowing stream.

"We should have done this earlier," Beck shouted as he struggled to close a shutter. He had to shout, because of the roar of the wind.

"It's going to get worse, I'm afraid," Andrews shouted back.

When the shutters were secured, the men went back inside, taking the chairs with them. Arabella and Maggie were bringing food in from the kitchen.

"I know it's a little early," Arabella said as she placed the food on the table. "But if this storm gets worse, we may not get a chance to eat later."

"It's not too early for me," Beck said.

"Elmer, if someone woke you at three o'clock in the morning, it wouldn't be too early for you," Andrews teased.

"This is a frightening storm," Mrs. Emma Rittenhouse said as she came down the stairs. She was a 71 year old widow, who had lived at the Red House from the time it had been built.

"It's more than just a storm," Beck said. "This is a hurricane."

"Ahh, it won't 'mount to much," Bowman said. "I'm 82 years old, 'n I've been through a lot of hurricanes. They don't never do all that much damage here. I think it's 'cause we are an island, 'n they most just pass over us 'n do the worst on the mainland."

"I've been through a few myself, Mr. Bowman, although I've not been through one in Galveston," Arabella replied. "It seems this one gained strength quite quickly."

"You went through them New Orleans hurricanes. I expect they're different here. Don't never do much damage."

Arabella smiled as she glanced out the one window that had been left uncovered. "I hope you're right."

As the boarders, five men and two women, as well as Cade, Arabella, and Maggie ate their dinner, they engaged in a banter between them, forcing the conversation perhaps to overcome their nervousness.

"Maggie, what'd you say this stuff is?" Beck asked.

"Veal cordon bleu."

"Blue, huh?" Beck replied. "It don't look blue, but I tell you what, it could be pure purple far as I'm concerned. This is real good."

All the while they were having their dinner, the sounds from outside were growing louder, and more alarming. In addition to the roar of the wind and the drumming of the rain, they heard a loud, crashing sound.

"What was that?" Mrs. Rittenhouse asked.

"It sounded like a tree falling," Andrews said.

"Or a building collapsing," Cline added.

"I don't know," Bowman said, nervously. "Maybe this storm is bigger than what I remember."

Joan Baker stood up. "I'm going down to the orphanage while I can still get there. Sister Anna Kathleen will more than likely need me to help with the children."

Although Joan wasn't a nun, she was a very devout person, and she often did volunteer for the St. Cecilia orphanage.

"Are you sure you want to do that?" Arabella asked. "Just look out there."

"I feel I should," Joan said. "All the sisters are old and I know I can be of help."

"Well, if you're going, you can't go by yourself," Cade said as he rose from the table. "Elmer, help me open the shutters so we can get out."

"Thanks, Cade."

With Joan holding on to his arm, Cade held Joan close to him as they walked down the street, fighting the wind and the rain. Water had already spilled out of Q Street and continued to rise so that by the time they reached the orphanage, it was ankle deep.

Cade had to knock very loudly on the door before it was opened by Sister Anna Kathleen.

"Oh, Joan, I knew you would be here!" she said. "Bless you. Bless you, my child! Come in. Let me get you out of those wet clothes before you catch your death of cold. You, too, Mr. McCall."

"I'd better not," Cade said. "I need to get back to the Red House and see how those folks are faring, but if you need anything, send Alvaro to get me."

"Poor Alvaro. Before he came here, he lived down on the coast," Sister Anna Kathleen said shaking her head. "His mother, bless her soul, was killed in a storm like this, and now he's in the chapel in prayer."

"It seems to me like that would be a good place to be," Cade said. "I'll come and see about you tomorrow."

"We'll appreciate that," Joan said.

Cade made his way back to the boarding house, leaning into the wind. The water was much higher now than it had been when he started out, and by the time he got back, all five steps leading up to the porch were submerged. The wind was blowing so hard that he had to hang onto one of the support posts. Turning to look back, he saw a large object rolling down the street. It careened into a light post, and snapped it off, the wind immediately flinging the post into the air. The post was coming toward the porch and like a missile, it hit the shutter causing it to splinter into a hundred pieces. Just then the original object started to move, and Cade saw that it was the roof of a house, or at least part of a roof. More debris—wooden timbers, shingles, tin, bricks—all were flying through the air, slamming against the walls of houses and buildings, like shot fired from cannon. Down the street, Cade could see wreckage piling up between two houses creating a dam that caused the water to back up. It seemed to Cade as if the storm was increasing in strength and the water getting deeper with the passing of each minute.

Cade saw an empty box wagon, floating down the street like a rapidly moving boat. Leaving the street it started toward the house but missed it. The wagon slammed up against a submerged limb from the live oak tree that stood between The Red House, and the building next door. The limb held the wagon in place wedging it against the tree. By now the Red House was surrounded by water.

Cade forced the door opened, the wind catching it and jerking it out of his hands. The glass shattered. When he tried to close it, he found that he couldn't push it against the wind. Beck and French, seeing that he was having trouble came over to assist him, and it took all three to get the shutters back in place and the door closed.

"Did you make it to the orphanage?" Arabella asked as she hurried to Cade.

"I did."

"I don't know why Joan thought she had to go down there. She should have stayed right here where she would be dry," Arabella said.

"None of us is going to be dry for very long," Beck said. "Look, water's already coming in through the door and under it, too."

"Oh, it's going to ruin my rug," Arabella said dropping to her knees to pull back the carpet.

"I'm afraid it's going to do a lot more than ruin the carpet," Cade said. "There's a dam down the street and it's causing the water to back up fast. We need to all move upstairs, if we're going to ride this thing out."

Almost as soon as Cade said the words, there was a terrible, cracking sound as the wind ripped off the roof and the back wall began to buckle. Water was gushing in.

"We're gonna die! We're gonna die!" Maggie screamed.

"No we're not," Arabella yelled as she took Maggie by the shoulders and began to shake her. "Cade's here. He'll take care of us."

"If you have any ideas, now's the time to tell us," Andy French said, his voice high-pitched with fright. "There ain't no upstairs to get to."

The entire house began to shake.

"Oh! Jesus! What's happening?" Maggie cried out.

The shaking lasted but a few seconds, then the house was pushed from its foundation, not by wind, but by a tidal surge. The abrupt movement of the house caused everyone but Cade and Beck to fall into the water. Quickly they got the others back on their feet.

"This entire house is about to be swept away," Cade said, raising his voice against the roar of wind and water. "We have to get out of here!"

"How are we going to do that?" Andrews asked. "Look." Andrews pointed to the front door which was now at the top of a steep incline, the result of the house having shifted. "Even if we could get up to the door, it would be a long drop."

"We can't go out the back either," Cline said. "What's left of the roof and back wall has us blocked in."

"Cade, the window! Can we climb out of it?" Arabella pointed to the un-shuttered window on the side of the house.

Clambering up the incline Cade looked out the window. The wagon he had seen earlier was still jammed up against the tree.

"Arabella's right," Cade called. "There's a wagon bed stuck in a tree. If we can get to it we've got a chance."

"I don't think we can do that, especially the older folks and the women," Andy French said when he got to where Cade was standing.

"Maybe we can't make it," Mrs. Rittenhouse said. "But I'm too old to be entombed in a pile of rubble when this house comes crashing down." The old woman began crawling up the incline.

"Cade, have you got a line?" Beck asked. "I can go first and secure the line so the others will have a hand hold when they try to get to the wagon."

"Good idea, I've got some rope in my room," Cade replied. "That is if my room is still there."

Cade's room was on the first floor at the back of the house. When he got to it, he saw that the back wall had collapsed inward making it very difficult to enter. Getting down on his hands and knees, he managed to pass under the collapsed wreckage until he reached the wall where he had kept two coils of rope hanging from hooks. The problem was that in this part of the room the back wall was so low that he couldn't even crawl under it.

He was about to give up when he got an idea. The water on the floor of his room was at least two feet high, but turning over onto his back, he went under water, and pushed himself beneath the wreckage. He knew that he was taking a great risk, because any additional shift in the house could keep him trapped here.

He opened his eyes, and though he couldn't see the ropes, he could see the leg of the chest which was held down by the wall and the roof. He knew that the ropes were hanging on hooks just to the right of the chest, and he reached up for them.

The first thing he discovered was that he would only be able to reach one of them. The second thing he discovered was that no matter how he tried to jiggle the rope, it was wedged in by the same wall that was holding the chest, and he couldn't flip it off the hook. His only hope of getting the rope free would be to pull it hard enough to jerk the retaining hook out of the wall. And, because he could only get one hand on the rope, that would make it even harder. He gave a quick prayer of thanks that it was his right, and not his left hand that could reach it, then he started pulling.

At first there was no movement at all, then he thought he felt something. Had he? Or was this merely wishful thinking? No, there was definite movement, if he could just stay here long enough.

Cade had been under water for so long now that he could feel the increasing ache in his lungs from holding his breath. He desperately wanted air, but he was afraid that if he abandoned his position to take a breath, he might not be able to get back.

He had to stay here.

Cade gave one more hard yank on the rope, and he felt it come loose. Quickly he pushed himself out from under the collapsed wall, then raised up. But now the water was so deep that he couldn't put his head above water while still sitting. He stood up, gasping for breath.

The water was now almost to his waist, and he started working his way through it, back to the common room. There, he saw the panic-stricken faces of all who had been waiting for him.

"I've got the rope!" Cade said with a triumphant smile.

He tied one end of the rope off to an exposed stud, then he gave the other end to Beck. "Here you go."

The wind was strong and the water, which was now chest deep on Beck, was still rising. He had a difficult time but he managed to cross the space to the wagon. Once there, he secured the rope to the front wheel and then the back tying it off to the axel.

"Send the first one over!" he shouted, his voice tinny against the roar of wind and rushing water. Tree limbs, pieces of collapsed houses, and other debris was whipping by both afloat, and in the air.

"Arabella, get going," Cade said moving her toward the window.

"When are you coming?" Arabella asked.

"I'll wait until everybody is out."

"I'm staying with you."

A pained expression crossed Cade's face. "You have to go," he pleaded.

"No."

"All right," Cade said. He had to admit, he admired her courage and determination. He turned toward Maggie. "It's up to you. You have to show everybody how to do this."

"Arabella, I'm going to die. I know I'm going to die," Maggie said, too frightened to move.

"No you aren't," Arabella replied. "Magnolia, you're the only family I've got. I won't let you die."

"You can do this, Maggie," Cade said. "You've got to do it, for the others. The water is too deep to walk, so don't even try. Just stretch out, grab hold of the rope, and pull yourself across to the wagon." Cade helped her through the window. She did as Cade had instructed, and when she reached the wagon, Beck pulled her in, balancing it so that it didn't tip over.

Cade helped the others through the window, and all including Mrs. Rittenhouse, made it to the wagon bed. Lee Bowman had declined every opportunity to leave until now only he, Arabella and Cade remained.

"Mr. Bowman, you're next."

"I can't go out there," Bowman said.

"You can't stay here, the water is getting higher and this whole building is going to collapse at any moment."

"I can't move," Bowman said.

"Arabella, you go," Cade said. "I'll bring Mr. Bowman."

By now the water was considerably higher, and even with the rope, Arabella had a difficult time negotiating the distance between the house and the wagon bed, but she was able to do so.

"All right, Mr. Bowman there are just the two of us. Let's go."

Cade climbed out first and holding on to the rope with one hand, he reached the other hand up to grab Bowman. But just as he did so, a tidal surge came through and the rest of the house was swept away, Bowman going with it. That also took out the rope that was tied to the stud as the force of the collapsing house dislodged the wagon bed from the tree.

Cade looked around for Mr. Bowman but couldn't find him, then he realized that he, too, was being swept away. When he looked toward the wagon bed, he saw that it was beginning to move swirling rapidly through the other debris. Without the rope to help, he started toward where he thought the wagon bed would be, fighting the current, as he tried to swim against it.

"Cade! Take the line!" Beck shouted. Having drawn the rope back in, he now threw it toward Cade. The rope hung up on a snag of a tree, and Cade was able to make his way to it. Holding onto the rope, Beck and French were able to maneuver the wagon to Cade pulling him in where he lay collapsed on the floor.

"Ever' body grab a' hold of somethin'!" Beck shouted. "We're in for a wild ride!" They were now adrift, part of the flotsam that was being whipped along by the rushing water.

"Everybody look out for Mr. Bowman," Cade said between gasps of air. He raised his head to look toward where he had last seen the old man, but even the house was out of sight.

4

The rain and the strong wind stopped at about one o'clock. The stillness was stark as the residents of The Red House huddled together waiting for the first light of day.

"Will you look at this," Cade said when he could make out where they were.

The wagon that had served as their makeshift boat was lodged in the branches of an uprooted magnolia tree.

"Oh this poor tree," Mrs. Rittenhouse said. "I hope it's not the one that was in Miss O'Hara's yard."

"If it hadn't been for this tree, we very well could be in the Gulf, and we may not be floating, at least not in this wagon, but right now, I've got to get out of this thing." David Andrews said, making his way to a spot of dry ground.

"Me, too," Maggie said as she grabbed onto a branch of the tree. It was then that she began screaming.

"It's over," Arabella soothed. "Everything's fine."

But Maggie continued to scream as she withdrew her hand from the tree branch.

Cade found that snakes had taken refuge in the downed tree just as they had. He jumped out into the water that had receded to below his knees. He coaxed Maggie into his arms

33

and carried her to the island Andrews had found. Arabella, French, Cline, and Beck, who was carrying Mrs. Rittenhouse, joined the other three.

"It's eerie," Arabella said. "Do you think we're the only ones left alive?"

"There are others," Cade said. "Look. Some buildings are completely gone, and others look almost untouched."

"Do you think we'll find Mr. Bowman?" Maggie asked.

No one answered her question.

The city of Galveston opened all the public buildings that had not been damaged by the hurricane, and made them available as temporary shelters to the people who had lost their homes. Many of the citizens left town, including all but three of those who had been residents in the Red House. Beck, the seaman, found a berth onboard a ship, while French and Mrs. Rittenhouse found sanctuary in one of the public buildings that had survived the storm. They did not know the whereabouts of Joan Baker.

One of the buildings that did not survive the storm was the Heckemeyer Stables, where Cade kept Barney. The building was destroyed, and twenty-one horses killed. Barney was one of the twenty-one.

Cade felt an intense sense of grief and loss over the death of his horse, but he also felt somewhat guilty about mourning the loss of a horse, when people had been killed.

"Oh, Cade, Barney?" Arabella said when Cade reported the loss.

Cade nodded, but didn't speak.

"He was such a sweet soul. I'm so sorry," Arabella said, embracing him.

"What will we do now?" Maggie asked. "We have no place to stay."

"Yes we do," Cade said.

There was only one place that Cade could think of to go, and that was to the ranch that he and Jeter Willis owned. The

MW was located about thirty-five miles from Galveston. It had two cabins, one that he and Jeter used when they were there, and the other was where Titus and Mary Hatley lived. The Hatleys had raised Jeter from the time he was five years old when his father had been shot and his mother had been abducted in an Indian raid. They were the "parents" who had raised Jeter, and one of the reasons he had wanted to buy the piece of land was to provide a home for the elderly couple.

When Cade inquired, he found that the railroad bridge had been damaged in the storm, and there would be no way of getting off the island except by boat. He and Arabella and Maggie went down by the dock to see if the Bell and Sail had survived, and to see if Stan Virden had a suggestion.

"Most of the small craft were pretty beaten up," Stan said. "It looks like we're all in this together, at least for a little while. If you want you can live here in the chandler shop for awhile. It won't be comfortable, but you'll be dry—at least you will be when I can get some boards to cover up that hole up there."

"We may have to do that," Cade said. "But there has to be a way to get to the mainland."

"Don't know why you'd want to. The wind didn't stop at the water's edge," Stan said. "I told you, ya gotta place here."

Cade looked up at the row of ships that had been in port. Anchored at the far wharf was the *Success*. It was very obvious that the ship was preparing to get underway.

"Wait here, for a moment," Cade said, walking down to where a gangplank ran from ship to shore.

"Permission to come aboard?" he called up.

"Wait," the sailor called back, as he left his position. When he returned a moment later, Cade saw that Pops was with him.

"Cade!" Pops called down, a big smile on his face. "I was wondering how you fared. Are you wanting to join the crew?"

"In a manner of speaking. May I come aboard?"

"Sure, come on up."

A few minutes later, Cade returned to where the two women were standing. "Come with me," he said. "I've got us passage to the mouth of the Navidad River."

Shortly after coming aboard, Pops opened the bosun's locker.

"It'll take you a while to get to your ranch won't it?"

"Yes, I'd say it will," Cade said.

"A seaman's garb may not be the most fashionable outfit you can pick, but it'll be dry. Here put these on." He handed them each a set of duck pants and a loose shirt.

During the brief voyage down the coast, Arabella and Maggie had been restricted to "officer's country" which was the quarter deck, while Cade earned their passage by working as an able-bodied seaman. He even went aloft to furl sails.

"See how it all comes back to you?" Pops said. "It's not too late—I can talk to the cap'n and sign you on."

"Thanks, Mr. Burke," Cade said, using the proper address to recognize Pop's rank. "But I think I'd better stay with the cattle."

The *Success* reached the mouth of the Navidad after being under way for less than three hours. It didn't put in, but Pops ordered a boat lowered to take Cade, Arabella and Maggie ashore. Cade climbed down the rope ladder first, so he would be in position to help the two ladies into the boat. This was necessary because both the rowboat and the ship were riding the swells, and sometimes the end of the ladder would be as high as six feet above the bottom of the boat.

Pops helped Arabella and Maggie onto the ladder, timing the swells as best he could. Then, when all three were in the boat, Pops leaned over to shout down.

"Good luck, Cade!"

"Thanks for the ride, Pops!" Cade called back. Now that he was no longer a temporary member of the crew, he felt no constraints about referring to his friend in such a familiar way.

"Potter, take these people to the beach!" Pops shouted to the sailor who was manning the boat.

"Aye, aye, sir," Potter called back, and as Cade released the line that held the small boat to the *Success*, the young sailor began to row.

When they stepped onto land at the mouth of the Navidad River, Cade saw at least a dozen unattended boats that had been deposited by the storm. Most were so damaged as to be useless, but he found one that looked seaworthy, and pushing it into the river, it proved to be watertight. After some searching, he also found some useable oars, then he called out to the other two.

"Climb aboard, mates, we're almost there."

"Mates?" Arabella replied. "All right, we sailed on the ship with you, but, mates?"

"Arrghhh," Cade replied in his best pirate imitation.

Arabella laughed. "We'd better get into the boat, Magnolia, or I fear he'll make us walk the plank or something."

Rowing upstream wasn't as difficult as Cade had initially thought it would be. That was because instead of a downriver current, the storm had caused the Navidad to spill over its banks, and it was now a wide pool of still water.

The farther up river they got, the less storm damage they saw, but even this far up, the river was still out of its banks, and because it was, the dock Cade had been looking for was no longer there. However, Cade was able to recognize the place where the MW landing should be and he put the boat in, then secured it to a tree.

"So, this is the MW," Arabella said as Cade helped her and Maggie out of the boat. "You've spoken about it, but this is the first time I've seen it."

"This is your ranch?" Maggie asked.

"Yes, well, mine and Jeter's. But we only have five hundred acres, so calling it a ranch is sort of putting on a bit of the dog."

"*Un peu du chien?*" Maggie asked.

Arabella laughed. "Not a *little* dog, a *bit* of the dog. It is an expression meaning exaggerating."

"Ah, I see," Maggie said, laughing with Arabella.

They had to walk a couple of hundred yards to reach the ranch and when they got there, they saw Jeter repairing a fence.

"Jeter," Cade yelled.

Jeter looked up at the sound of Cade's voice, and the expression on his face registered his surprise at seeing them.

"Cade? Arabella? What are you doing here?" Jeter asked. "And what are you doing afoot? Where's Barney?"

Cade paused for a moment before he responded. "Barney's dead. He was killed in the storm."

Jeter shook his head. "I know what a store you set by that horse. The storm was that bad, was it?"

"It was bad," Cade replied without getting into specifics. "It was bad enough that we're here seeking shelter."

"The Red House?"

"It's gone," Arabella said, the tone of her voice indicating her sense of loss. "This is Magnolia Trudeau, Jeter. She's been living with us."

Jeter nodded. "Glad to meet you ma'am."

Cade dropped the little bundle of clothes they had been wearing. "This is all we have left. The clothes we're wearing now came from the bosun's locker on the ship that brought us here."

"Damn, how bad was this storm?" Jeter asked.

"Galveston was hit pretty hard, but the worst thing is, the number of people who lost their lives. Nobody really knows how many, but it has to be at least a couple of hundred."

"Did you lose anybody you know?" Jeter asked.

"We watched one old man get washed away when the house floated out, and another woman who lived with us went to help out at an orphanage. We never heard from her, so we are assuming she is dead," Arabella said.

"That's too bad." Jeter was quiet for a moment, simply because he didn't know what else to say. Then he smiled. "I'll bet you folks are hungry."

"I'm so hungry I could eat the south end of a northbound horse," Cade said. "We haven't eaten since yesterday afternoon."

"Then come on up to the house. I know Ma's got a big pot of ham and beans on the back of the stove."

"How is Mary?" Cade asked.

"She's gettin' by," Jeter said. "Pa tries his best to see to her. Oh, I've put up another little cabin so we can hire somebody else to come take care of them and the place when we're trailing next spring."

"Is it finished?" Cade asked.

"Pretty much. I even built some furniture to go in it. Nothin' fancy, but a hand could use it."

"What about these two women? Is it big enough for them?"

Jeter rolled his eyes. "Probably not, but they could have our cabin and you and I could sleep in the henhouse."

"The henhouse?" Arabella asked.

"That's what Pa calls my cabin. He doesn't think too much of my skills as a carpenter. Come on. I'll show it to you," Jeter said as he picked up his tools and started toward the houses.

They went first to the Hatley's cabin. It had a large open room with red checked curtains at the windows.

"Ma, look who's here," Jeter said taking the old woman's hand. "It's Cade. He's come back and he wants some of your beans."

Cade leaned over and gave her a kiss on the forehead. "I can't wait, but tell me, do you have any cornbread?"

A large smile crossed her face. "Now tell me boy, can you have beans without cornpone? It's not hot, but you can crumble it up in some sweet milk, like you always do."

"You remembered," Cade said.

"Of course I remembered," Mary said. "It's my rheumatism that got me down, not my mind."

Cade laughed. "That's good. I've brought you some help that's going to stay here with you for a while. This is Arabella Dupree and this is Magnolia Trudeau."

"My, my, you're both pretty little things, but why are you wearing these ugly clothes?"

"A storm hit Galveston, and this is the best we could do," Arabella said.

"Can you sew?"

"No, but we can cook," Maggie said.

"That's good. Titus has to help me get around these days, and he thinks he's on a cattle drive again. All he ever wants is beans."

Arabella and Maggie were given Jeter and Cade's cabin, and Cade and Jeter moved into the new cabin. It was Jeter who, over breakfast the next morning, suggested that they go to Galveston to help with the cleanup, and Cade agreed.

"I'm willing to help in the cleanup," Cade said. "But while I'm there, I also intend to check in with the bank to see if our money is safe."

"Yes, good idea," Jeter agreed.

"Cade, Magnolia and I . . ." Arabella started to say, she hesitated for a moment before she continued. "I would never ask a man to do this, but Magnolia and I have no clothes to wear but the dresses we had on when the storm hit and these sailor clothes we're wearing now. Would you . . ."

Cade interrupted her with a little laugh. "You want me to buy you some new clothes."

"Yes, for Magnolia and me."

"I'll be glad to," Cade said with a rather salacious smile.

"Oh, and Cade? Do buy clothes we can be seen wearing in public."

"Well, now you are taking all the fun from it," Cade teased. "But I'll see what I can do."

Cade and Jeter reached Galveston by mid-afternoon where they were greeted with the stench of death from horses, cows, pigs, and family pets that were bloating in the street while flies swarmed over them. The bodies of the animals were floating in shallow pools, and hanging from trees. Every able-bodied man worked. The priority was in finding people who were alive, trapped under collapsed buildings or wandering around in shock. Dead bodies were recovered and animals were burned, and the smells permeated the air twenty-four hours per day. Cade was hoping he would find Mr. Bowman or Joan Baker, but he never found either of them.

Hotels and restaurants that could open their doors turned no one away. People who had lost their homes found shelter anywhere they could, in the train station, at the city hall, in commercial buildings, warehouses, saloons, and even whore houses. Finally, ten days after the storm, all the survivors had been accounted for and the dead had been buried. Now the city began to turn to the task of rebuilding.

One of the buildings that had been destroyed was the bank, and Cade was concerned about his money. He visited Charles Montgomery, the owner, at the site of the bank.

"We believe all the money is safe," Montgomery said in response to Cade's question. Montgomery pointed to the pile of bricks and sand where at least a dozen men were working. "The vault should be buried under all that rubble, and money that we had on deposit, as well as our records, are in the vault."

"I am assuming you will be rebuilding."

41

"Indeed we will," Montgomery said. "The merchants and the citizens of this town are going to be needing money and we at the First Galveston feel an obligation to meet that need. When Miss Dupree needs capital to rebuild The Red House, we'll be here for her—and for you, too, Mr. McCall."

Satisfied that his money was safe, even if he didn't have immediate access to it, Cade assured the banker that he would maintain his account and if the need arose, he would borrow money from the First Galveston.

The Saddle and Stirrup had been repaired and was now open for business. For the first time in several days, Cade and Jeter found an opportunity to relax for a while, and joined others that they knew for a beer.

"You think it's bad here," a cowboy named Art Finley said. Finley was one of the cowboys who had ridden with Cade and Jeter during the last cattle drive. "You should see it to the south of here. You think a lot of animals died in Galveston, well out on the range they's been hunnerts, maybe even thousands of cows that was kilt by the storm, now their carcasses are lyin' around, all over the place. You talk about stench. Whoeee!" Finley held his nose closed.

"I hadn't even thought about that," Cade said. "Of course, the cattle would have no place to shelter."

"Damn, I wonder if there'll even be a drive come spring," Jeter said.

"Good question," Cade replied. "We may wind up with a lean year, partner."

Cade and Jeter were ready to leave Galveston.

"Aren't you forgettin' somethin'?" Jeter asked.

"I don't think so."

"The clothes. Arabella told you to get her and Magnolia some dresses."

"Oh, yeah," Cade said as he stopped his horse in front of Blum's Mercantile. "Arabella used to shop here. Maybe someone can pick out what she'd like."

"You mean as much time as you spend with that woman, you don't know what she likes?"

That night the two women, wearing new dresses, prepared a feast of fried chicken for Cade and Jeter and the Hatleys. There was a great deal of conversation over the dinner table about the condition of Galveston, though Cade and Jeter downplayed the more gruesome aspects, concentrating instead on the willingness of so many to pitch in and help with the cleanup and rebuilding.

"Oh!" Arabella said, half-way through dinner. "I almost forgot. Mr. Puckett dropped by and he left a letter for you."

"Probably telling us he won't be needin' us for a cattle drive come spring," Jeter said.

Having left the table to retrieve the letter, Arabella came back a moment later with the missive in hand.

Cade and Jeter

As I'm sure you may know by now, thousands of cattle were killed by the hurricane, and there is a need for disposition of the dead animals. The hides can still be salvaged, but we will need men who are willing to do the hard work of skinning the cattle, then disposing of the carcasses. I will pay a dollar and a half per hide, cured and delivered to the LP Ranch. I hope you two men are interested in such a project.

I have been talking with other ranchers, and we think that if we merge our herds, we will have enough cattle for a spring drive. I have put forth you two men as contractors to manage the herd.

Linus Puckett

"Well, how about that?" Cade asked, as with a big smile he handed the letter to Jeter. "It looks like we aren't out of business just yet."

43

5

The next morning, as Cade and Jeter prepared to leave the MW, Arabella and Maggie joined them out by the corral. They were hitching a wagon to a team of mules, having decided not to take horses.

"Here's fifty dollars," Cade said as he handed the money to Arabella. "I wish I had more to give you, but until the bank is back in business you'll have to make this last. You can stay here or you can go back to Galveston."

"What's there to go back to?" Arabella asked. "Magnolia and I have discussed it, and we've decided we'd rather stay here with the Hatleys."

Cade smiled. "Good, I was hoping you would say that. But if you stay here, there's going to come a time when you will need more supplies. Texana is the closest town, and to get to it you just follow the river north for about five miles. Use Harry and Rhoda," Cade said, pointing out two of the horses. "They take to the harness easily, but Titus will help you hitch them up to the buckboard."

"When will you be back?" Arabella asked.

"I'm thinking not until sometime in the spring," Cade said. "You've got enough wood cut to last you until the end

44

of January, but you'll be needing some more to get you through the rest of the winter. Titus will want to do the cutting for you, but he's an old man so you help him. But you should start now, a little each day before it gets cold."

"The cabin you're in should stay warm because I've chinked a lot of mud into the cracks," Jeter said, "but if you have to move in with Ma and Pa then do it."

"*Merci,*" Maggie said, smiling at Jeter.

"Uh, yes, uhmm, well," Jeter said, clearing his throat in embarrassment over being the target of Maggie's direct stare. "Come on, Cade. We'd better be going."

Cade put his arms around Arabella and pulled her to him for a kiss.

"Monsieur, Jeter, do you not want a kiss goodbye?" Maggie asked.

"What?" Now Jeter's embarrassment left, to be replaced by a wide, elated smile. "Yes, of course I want a kiss goodbye."

Cade and Arabella looked on as Jeter kissed Maggie, though it would be more accurate to say that Maggie was kissing Jeter, as she had obviously taken the initiative.

The two young women stood side by side, waving as the wagon drew away from them.

"Monsieur Jeter is a very nice man," Maggie said.

"Are you beginning to . . . have feelings for him?" Arabella asked.

"Do you think it is wrong?"

"No more than it's wrong for me to have feelings for Cade. But Magnolia, remember who, and what we are."

"We are not the women we were in New Orleans. We have changed," Maggie insisted.

A sad expression crossed Arabella's face. "Unfortunately, we can't unring a bell, and we can't hide from who or what we are. No matter how much we want it to be different, we can't change our past."

"You don't think that Cade can forgive you? He knows who you are, and yet he seems to care for you," Maggie said.

"Magnolia, you don't know how much I want that to be true, but women like us can never change. It's a burden we will carry for the rest of our lives."

Because so many businesses had been destroyed by the hurricane, men who needed employment found skinning dead cows a means of survival. Store clerks, draymen, blacksmiths, people of all trades, were taking part in the cattle-hide business, along with Cade and Jeter.

"Tell me about Maggie," Jeter said one night while Cade and he were camped on Live Oak Bayou. Jeter was tending to a jack rabbit that was cooking over the fire.

"What do you mean, tell you about her? She's Arabella's friend; they worked together back in New Orleans."

"Worked together?"

"Yes, she was a whore, if that's what you're getting at," Cade said. "I've never asked what happened to her, but I get the feeling she left New Orleans in a hurry."

"Do you think she's running from something? Maybe the law?"

"Jeter Willis, you're the only person I know who's not running from something. Do you think for a minute I'm going back to Clarksville, Tennessee, anytime soon?"

"But that's different. Your brother married your fiancée when they thought you were killed in the war."

"That's true, but that's not the only reason I'm staying away," Cade said.

"All right, I won't ask anymore," Jeter said. "But let's get back to Magnolia. Don't you think she's sort of . . . well . . . I don't know how to say it, but she has sort of a different look about her. A good look, don't get me wrong, but it's sort of . . . different is the only word I can come up with."

"How about exotic?" Cade suggested.

"Exotic, yeah. But what does that mean?"

Cade chuckled. "It means just what you said: different, unusual, striking."

"Yeah, all that."

"Jeter, you do know she's a quadroon don't you?"

"No, I didn't know that."

"Does that make a difference?

"A difference how? What do you mean?"

"Does that make a difference about what you think about her?"

"I think she's one of the prettiest women I've ever seen, 'n I'd say that, no matter what she is."

"She is pretty," Cade agreed. "But she's no shrinking violet. I know that Arabella can take care of herself, and I think Maggie can, too."

"I hope you're right. I hated to leave them at the ranch, even if Ma and Pa are there with them."

Jeter couldn't help but think of Lilajean Willis. His father had left him and his mother alone, while he had gone out to hunt. When Lilajean saw Indians circling the cabin, she had put her five-year old son under a board in the floor and told him not to say anything or come out no matter what.

When he heard the sound of a gunshot, he thought it was his father coming home, but it was the shot that killed his father. No one came for him, and still he stayed under the floor in the dark. Finally, on the second day, he heard a sound and a banging on the board above him. Even though his mother had told him not to come out until she came for him, he moved the board aside. It was then that he saw her— bloodied and near death. She had escaped from her captors and come back for her son. He crawled out and sat beside her as she lay dying.

Two days later Titus Hatley came to borrow a gang plow.

It was then that Titus and Mary became his parents.

* * *

47

Four months later, and about a mile away from where
Cade and Jeter were working, a couple of men were engaged
in the same temporary occupation.

"Sum bitch!" Tyrone Grimes said. "I don't wish nothin'
bad for nobody, but we're goin' to wind up makin' more
money out 'a these here dead cows than we've ever made out
'a live ones."

"Yeah," Bart Canfield agreed. "I figure we got us at least
a hunnert 'n fifty dollars apiece there."

"Who's this comin' toward us?" Grimes asked, his voice
registering his apprehension as he watched four men
approach.

"I don't know. Maybe it's just somebody wantin' to be
friendly."

"Wait a minute, I know one o' them men," Canfield said.
"That's Amon Kilgore; he's a trail boss."

The two men waited as Kilgore and the three men with
him approached.

"Hello, boys," Kilgore said.

"Mr. Kilgore, what can we do for you?" Canfield asked.

Kilgore looked surprised that he was recognized. "You
know me?"

"Yeah, you're a trail boss. Took the Rocking D up last
year. I tried to sign on with ya but you turned me down."

"That's too bad."

"It don't make no never mind, mister. I hired on to the
Lazy 8."

"This ain't about herding cows. It's too bad you
recognized me because now I have to kill you."

"Now look, Kilgore, I ain't done nothin' to you,"
Canfield pleaded.

"It's not what you did, it's what you're gonna do."
Kilgore drew his pistol.

Canfield threw up his hand. "I got a wife and kids. You
can't just shoot me for nothin'."

"I'm takin' your hides, and I don't want nobody tellin' the law who done it."

Just then Tyrone Grimes started running for a copse of trees. One of the other men with Kilgore took aim and shot him.

"Damn, Pogue, you shot him in the back."

Pogue nodded his head as he turned his gun toward Canfield. "We thank ya' for all the work you've done,"

"If you're going to do this, get it over with," Canfield said as he stared into the man's eyes.

A satanic smile crossed Pogue's lips as he pulled the trigger.

"All right, that's done," Kilgore said. "Morgan, you and Cooper tie a rope to those hides and let's drag 'em over to the wagon."

"Did you hear something?" Jeter asked.

"Yeah, I heard it," Cade said. "Sounded like gunshots."

"It's probably Tyrone and Bart shootin' at something. I know they're pretty close to us," Jeter suggested.

"You're probably right. Maybe we should ride over and make sure everything's all right."

"I'll bet it's a coyote comin' after a carcass they didn't burn," Jeter said. "One thing's for sure, it's not Indians."

Cade laughed. "You're right about that. With all the cow skinners out here, if we all banded together we'd have an army. How many hides do we have in that pile?"

"This one makes five-hundred-fifty-two," Jeter said as he threw another one onto the wagon.

"Are you about ready to call it quits?" Cade asked. "With so many men out here scouring the coast, the cows we can find now are few and far between."

"And we've already taken five-hundred back to Mr. Puckett," Jeter said. "I say we head for home."

"I'm with you. It's turned out to be a pretty good winter," Cade said as he began kicking dirt onto the remaining embers left from the burning of the last carcass.

About half a mile away from Cade and Jeter's temporary encampment, Amon Kilgore, stood on a small rise, looking down toward the fire, wagon, and two men.

"How many hides do you think they got?" Morgan asked.

"I don't know, but they've got a wagon full, that's for sure," Kilgore replied. He was studying the site through a pair of binoculars. "And what's even more important, they got 'em loaded, so we can get out of here in a hurry." He lowered the binoculars, but he didn't move.

"Well, are we gonna' do it or not?" Julius Cooper asked.

"I know them two," Kilgore said. "That's Cade McCall and Jeter Willis."

"So what?" Cooper asked.

"I don't want them to see me."

"What difference does it make whether you're seen by them two or not? That poor bastard Pogue just killed knew you, too, and what did it get him? He's just as dead as the other one."

"These two are different," Kilgore said. "They're not goin' to be that easy to kill."

"That's all right, you just stay back here, like a puss 'n we'll kill 'em for you," Pogue said with an evil smile.

Cade and Jeter were striking their camp, when they saw three riders coming toward them.

"I wonder who these men are?" Jeter asked.

"I don't know, but I guess we're about to find out," Cade said. He was just about to put his bedroll into the back of the wagon, but he hung onto it as he watched the riders approach.

"Do you recognize any of them?" Cade asked.

"No, I don't."

The three men came on into the camp.

"I see you two boys have been busy this winter," One of the three riders said. "Your wagon looks pretty full there. How many hides do you have?"

"I don't see that it's any of your business," Cade answered.

"Here now, is that any way to respond to a friendly question?"

"Under the circumstances, I'm not sure the question is all that friendly," Cade replied.

"Well now, you may have a point there," the talkative rider said. "It turns out that there is a point to my question. I'm interested in how many hides you have, 'cause I plan to take 'em off your hands."

"They're not our hides to sell," Cade replied. "We're contracted to Linus Puckett for these hides."

The talkative rider chuckled. "Oh, you don't understand. I didn't say I was goin' to buy 'em. What I said was, that I plan to take 'em off your hands. You've not only done the job of skinning the cattle, you've even loaded them in the wagon for me."

"How do you plan to do that?" Cade asked.

"Easy enough. There ain't neither of you wearin' guns, but we are. That means that when we take your hides, there ain't nothin' you can do about it."

"I don't think I would like that," Cade said.

"Hear that boys? He ain't happy with our proposal." The talkative one reached for his pistol. "Let's just shoot 'em and ' be done with it."

The three men started for their pistols, but they were shocked when Cade dropped the bedroll to reveal a pistol in his hand.

"You boys don't really want to do that, do you?" Cade asked.

All three took their hands away from their pistols.

"Hold on there, now, just wait a minute!" the talkative one said. "You ain't really goin' to shoot us, are you?.

51

"Why not? You were about to shoot us."

"No, we wasn't really plannin' on actually shootin' you. I was just tellin' you that so's we could take your hides. But now that you got the drop on us, we'd be willin' to just ride away, 'n let you be. I mean, you couldn't actual just shoot us now, could you? Shootin' three men down in cold blood?"

"Mister, I think there's something you should know," Cade said. "During the war, I killed a lot of men, good men, husbands, fathers, sons, and the only reason I killed them was because they were wearing a different color uniform. Now if I could kill decent men like that, do you think, for one minute, that I wouldn't kill three low-life sons of bitches like you?"

"I told you, we wasn't really plannin' on shootin' you. We was just goin' to rob you is all."

"Get out of here," Cade said, making a waving motion with his pistol.

"We're goin', we're goin'," the talkative rider said and turning his horse, he, and the other two men rode off.

Cade and Jeter watched the would-be robbers until they were at least a quarter of a mile away.

"You drive," Cade said as the two men climbed into the wagon

Cade looked onto the floor under his feet and saw that the Henry repeating rifle was there. He picked it up and held it at his side.

"What are you doing that for?" Jeter asked.

The words were no sooner out of his mouth than they heard the buzz of a bullet, followed by the sound of gunfire.

Turning in his seat Cade saw the three men galloping toward them, pistols blazing away.

"Stop the wagon," Cade said.

"Are you serious?"

"We aren't going to be able to outrun them, and this will give me a stable firing platform."

The three were within pistol range, and the bullets continued to fly by, but because they were shooting from the back of galloping horses, the gunfire wasn't very accurate.

Cade raised the rifle to his shoulder and fired, jacked a round into the chamber and fired a second time, then repeated it to fire a third time. All three of the would-be robbers were down.

Kilgore had watched the entire operation from within a small thicket, the cottonwood trees providing him with enough concealment to prevent him from being seen.

It was too bad that they hadn't been able to get the hides from McCall and Willis. Inexplicably, Kilgore smiled. On the other hand, he had almost three hundred hides that they had taken from Canfield and Grimes, and now he didn't have to share them with anyone.

6

It was mid-afternoon by the time Cade and Jeter reached the LP Ranch with their load of cowhides. But it wasn't the cowhides that attracted everyone's attention. Tied to the back of the wagon were three horses, and draped across the horses were the bodies of the three outlaws who had tried to rob them.

"Damn," one of Puckett's cowboys said as he examined the bodies. "These here three men is Pogue, Morgan 'n Cooper."

"You know them, Slim?" Cade asked.

"Yeah we rode together some for the Bar J brand, but Mr. Jamison fired all three of 'em when he caught 'em stealin' some of his cows. They warn't no good."

"They's a reward out for 'em," one of the other cowboys said. "A hunnert dollars apiece. I seen the posters last time I was in Texana. Didn't say 'Dead or Alive' though, so I don't know if the reward will be paid or not."

"I expect we'll find out when we go to Texana," Cade said.

Texana, which was the nearest town to the MW ranch, had mail and stage routes, a growing business section, and its own newspaper, the *Clarion*. It was a busy shopping day when Cade and Jeter drove the wagon into town, and the boardwalks on either side of the street were filled. The sight of three horses, with bodies lying belly down across the saddle, caught the attention of everyone, and many began walking down the street rapidly enough to keep pace with the slowly moving wagon. By the time the entourage reached the middle of town, Sheriff Boskey had already been notified, and he was standing out in front of his office waiting to greet them.

"Jeter, Cade," the sheriff said, "who you bringin' in?"

"We're not sure," Cade admitted. "But a couple of Colonel Puckett's men said their names were Pogue, Morgan and Cooper."

"Pogue, Morgan and Cooper?" Sheriff Boskey stepped out into the street to take a look at the bodies, and grabbing them by the hair, he lifted each head for a closer examination.

"Yep, that's them all right," Sheriff Boskey said after he looked at all three bodies. "Keith Pogue, Sam Morgan and Julius Cooper. How'd you come by them?"

Cade and Jeter told the story of the run in with the three men. When they had finished, the sheriff told them about finding Grimes and Canfield's bodies.

"I expect these were the ones who killed those two men, only there was no trace of their hides," the sheriff said.

"I suspect there may have been a fourth one," Cade added.

"Did you get a look at him?"

"No. It's just something that I felt. I can't explain it."

"You don't have to. I know what it's like to get a notion," Sheriff Boskey said. "But you did wind up with three men, and they're worth a hundred apiece, so if you'll come to the bank with me, I'll authorize the payment."

Amon Kilgore sold 312 hides and had a little over two hundred and thirty dollars in his pocket when he rode into Victoria. The town was full of activity, and young men, who Kilgore took to be cowboys, scurried around like ants at a picnic. Nearly all of them were armed, and Kilgore was certain it was all for show.

Dismounting in front of the Last Chance Saloon, Kilgore looped the reins around the hitching post then went inside. He had picked up a copy of the *Texana Clarion*, because there had been an article in the paper that caught his interest. After buying a whiskey, he found an empty table and sat there to reread it.

HERDS TO BE JOINED FOR CATTLE DRIVE

The unwelcome arrival of the hurricane of September past visited coastal Texas with terrible effect. Particularly hard hit was Galveston, where there was great loss of life and property. But Brazora, Matagorda, and Jackson counties were also visited by the storm, and as a consequence, several thousand cows were killed.

Many of the ranchers have been able to avoid a total economic loss by harvesting the hides of the deceased animals. But, so severe was the reduction in livestock that there was some concern that there would be no cattle drive this year, as in previous shipping seasons. That would have created a serious loss of revenue among the cattle owners, had Colonel Linus Puckett of the LP Ranch not come up with an idea that might prove to be the salvation of the cattlemen of the region.

It is Colonel Puckett's idea to have several ranchers combine their herds so that they may share the expenses of the drive. It is estimated that there will be as many as twenty-five hundred or more bovines expected to head north. Because of the loss of so many cows in the storm, the price of cattle at the railhead is now thirty-five dollars per head. This is about twice as much as the average cow brought last year,

56

and the inordinately high payment will be a welcome relief to those cattlemen who, so recently faced economic disaster.

And, as before, Colonel Puckett has hired the contracting company of McCall and Willis to manage the drive.

Kilgore smiled, as he read the article. "Well, Mr. McCall and Mr. Willis, I'm not through with you yet." He gave voice to the words, though he spoke quietly, lest someone would hear him.

"Well I'll be damn, if it ain't my old friend, Emil Harmon," someone said and looking up from his newspaper, Kilgore saw a man he recognized.

"The name is Kilgore, Amon Kilgore." He rose and extended his hand. "It's been a long time, Taylor."

"The name is Toombs," Taylor replied, a broad smile crossing his face. "Fred Toombs."

Emil Harmon and Billy Taylor had served together in the 18th Infantry, under Colonel Carrington. But the two men, who were thought to be perennial trouble makers, killed the sergeant who was in charge of their punishment detail, then deserted. They went their separate ways after leaving the Montana Territory, Harmon taking the name Kilgore, and Taylor, the name Toombs.

"What are you doin' in Victoria?" Toombs asked.

"Just passin' through. What about you? You livin' here now?"

"Yeah, I got a job at the stables."

"You don't say? The stables? Do you like your job?"

"Hell no, I don't like it. Harmon, you know as well as anybody what it was like pullin' stable duty in the army. This ain't no different."

"The name's Kilgore."

"Yeah, Kilgore, I'll remember that."

"See that you do." Kilgore looked back down at the newspaper, then glanced back up at Toombs. "Would you be interested in somethin' I'm plannin'?"

"If what you got in mind don't require shovelin' shit, I'm all for it."

"We'll need to round up a few more men. But I'm new in these parts. Do you know anyone who might be interested?

"Yeah," Toombs said. "Yeah, I've got a few ideas."

"Bring 'em around, let me talk to 'em."

"What you plannin'?" Toombs asked. "The reason I ask is, if I know it, it might help me get some others."

"There don't nobody need to know 'til I'm ready for 'em to know. It's like you said, it don't require shovelin' shit," Kilgore replied.

"That's good enough for me," Toombs said.

Leaving the saloon, Kilgore worked up a good spit of tobacco and squirted it onto the boardwalk. Although he hadn't intended to do so, it got on the boots and pants cuff of a young cowboy who was just passing by. A young woman walking with the cowboy just managed to avoid it.

"Hey, mister, you just spit on my boots!" the cowboy complained.

Kilgore looked at the cowboy, then glanced down to the man's boots. "Yeah," he said. "It looks like I did do that, don't it?" He started to untie his horse.

"Leave your horse be, mister. Least wise 'till you get this took care of," the cowboy challenged

"What do you mean, 'till I get that took care of'?"

"What I mean is, I plan for you to come over here 'n clean your tobacco spit offen my boot."

"Just go on your way, boy," Kilgore said. "Showin' off for the woman here ain't worth gettin' yourself kilt."

The girl pulled on the cowboy's arm. "Come on, Bobby, let's go. I'll clean it."

"No," Bobby said. "This scoundrel made the mess, he's the one who's gonna clean my boot."

"Sonny, why don't you listen to your whore, and just pass on by?" Kilgore said.

"Whore?" the young woman gasped.

"I don't know where you're from, you pig-faced son of a bitch, but I'm callin' you out!" the young cowboy said, his voice cracking in anger.

"No, wait, Bobby, please!" the young girl pleaded. "It's all right. Come on, please? Let's go!"

Bobby put his hand on the butt of his pistol.

"You know what? You spittin' on my boot don't matter no more. Now I'm goin' to kill you for callin' my girl a whore. No, I'm goin' to kill you, just 'cause I don't like your looks. I'm going to count to three, then you go for your gun."

"Bobby, no!" the young woman said, her words now on the verge of a scream.

By now, half-a-dozen passers-by had been drawn to the scene by the loud talk.

"Who's that feller Bobby Sinclair is bracin'?" one of them asked.

"I don't know who the feller is, more 'n likely he's new in town 'n don't know who it is he's standin' up to., Sinclair's done kilt hisself three men, you know. He's awfully fast."

"He's murdered three, you mean."

"No, they was standin' up, face to face fights."

"It was the same as murder. There warn't none of 'em as fast as Sinclair, 'n he knowed it when he pushed 'em into the fight."

"I don't know about this man, though. He don't look none too scared of Bobby."

'That's just cause he don't know who Bobby Sinclair is."

Bobby Sinclair and Amon Kilgore were oblivious to the conversations taking place around them.

"Mary, step on out of the way," Bobby said.

"Miss, you better get on over here," one of the onlookers said. "There's goin' to be shootin' for sure, 'n you don't want to be in the way."

"What's it going to be, mister?" Bobby challenged. "Are you going to apologize to the lady? Or do I start counting?"

"You're goin' to die, boy," Kilgore said, flashing an evil grin.

This wasn't going as Bobby had planned. He was good with a gun, but he just realized that he wasn't going to be good enough. That realization had come too late. It was impossible for him to back out now, without spending the rest of his life in shame, and that, he couldn't do.

Bobby licked his lips a couple of times, then, with a voice that was much less authoritative than it had been when he started this confrontation, he began to count.

"One," he said. He paused for a long time, praying that, somehow this could all go away, that this man he had challenged would apologize, or at least, turn and walk away. The man continued to look at him with a cold, unblinking stare.

"Two."

Kilgore drew his pistol and fired, the bullet plunging into the center of Bobby's chest. Bobby looked at him with a shocked expression on his face,

"I . . . didn't . . . say . . . three." He put his hand over the wound, and blood spilled through his fingers.

"Yeah, well, I got tired of waitin' around," Kilgore said. He was talking to a man he had just shot, but the tone of his voice showed neither excitement, nor remorse.

The young man, his pistol still in his holster, collapsed.

"Bobby!" Mary shouted, and pulling away from the person who tried to hold her back, she rushed to Bobby's side, looking down in his face just as he breathed his last.

"What's goin' on here?" an authoritative voice shouted. "Make way, make way, let me through."

Kilgore, with the smoking pistol still in his hand, looked up to see a man pushing his way through the crowd. He was wearing a star.

"You're too late, Deputy Reynolds," one of the men said.

"Is that Sinclair?" Deputy Reynolds asked, pointing to the man laying half on, and half off the board walk."

"Yeah, it is."

"It was a fair fight, Deputy," one of the others said. "Sinclair egged it on."

"Are you saying this fella drew his gun faster 'n Sinclair did?"

There was no immediate response from those who had gathered to watch the fight.

"The truth is, Deputy, I didn't give 'im a chance to draw his gun," Kilgore said. "He commenced to countin', 'n he told me he was goin' to kill me when he got to three. So I figured 'bout the only chance I had was to shoot him before he got to three."

"Yeah," one of the onlookers said. "Yeah, Deputy, that's exactly the way it happened."

"What about you, Miss Webster?" Reynolds asked the young woman who was now sitting on the boardwalk crying quietly. "Did Sinclair bring on this fight?"

Mary nodded. "Yes," she said, speaking so quietly that she could barely be heard.

"Come with me to see the judge," Deputy Reynolds said. "I'll tell 'im what folks is sayin', 'n I expect he'll say there won't be any charges. Hell, he'll prob'ly thank you for killin' Sinclair. He ain't been nothin' but trouble since he was a sprout."

True to Deputy Reynolds' prediction, Judge Broome declared that it was a case of *minari mortem alicui*, meaning the "threat of death". This was validated by the witnesses therefore there was no cause to ask the grand jury for indictment. As a result Amon Kilgore was released, with no charges.

7

As Amon Kilgore stepped up to the bar in the Last Chance Saloon, the bar tender spoke to him.

"I done heard that the judge said you wasn't at fault for killin' Sinclair and to tell you the truth, Sinclair ain't no big loss anyhow. But I'd appreciate it if somebody comes in here to brace you, you'd take it outside into the street. It ain't good for business to have gunfights in here."

Kilgore responded to the admonition by glaring at the bartender. He spoke not a word, but no words were needed, and the bartender, made uneasy by the scowl, hurried down to the other end of the bar.

Using the mirror behind the bar, he perused the rest of the saloon. There were three young bar-girls working the customers, inveigling them to buy drinks with the promise of more than just conversation, a promise that would be unfulfilled unless the men were inclined to part with more money. One of the girls, seeing that Kilgore was watching her in the mirror, approached him with a practiced grin.

"My, aren't you the quiet one though, standing over here all by yourself."

Kilgore took a swallow of his beer, but he didn't respond.

"I saw you watching me in the mirror," the girl said.

"I was looking at all of you," Kilgore said.

The girl's smile broadened. "Well, you can talk."

"I can talk.

"You have to have company to talk," the girl said. "Buy me a drink, and I'll be company for you."

"Later," Kilgore said. "Right now I'm waiting for a business partner."

"Well, when your business is done, my name is Blissful," the girl said. "You won't forget now, will you?"

"I'll remember."

He watched the girl walk away, wishing he could go upstairs with her right now. This Sinclair wasn't the first man he had killed, but after he had killed, he needed a woman to take his mind off what he had done.

But right now he was having a run of bad luck. He'd gambled away almost all the money he'd got for the cow hides, and now he was down to his last twenty dollars. But if everything worked out, that would soon change. The article in the newspaper had said that McCall and Willis would be taking a herd to the rail head in Kansas.

"Some of 'em ain't goin' to get there," Kilgore mused.

Fred Toombs and two other men pushed through the batwing doors. He brought the men up to the bar.

"These here is . . ." Toombs started, but Kilgore interrupted him.

"Not here. Barkeep, I'll have another beer, and give these three men one, on me."

"I'd rather have whiskey," one of the men said.

"I ain't goin' to spend more 'n a nickel on you 'till I know you better," Kilgore replied. "You want whiskey, you'll pay for it yourself."

"I'll have a beer," the man said, amending his order.

Kilgore left twenty cents on the bar, then, as the men were waiting to be served he walked toward an empty table in the far back corner. He took his seat at the table, with his back against the corner wall, and waited until Toombs and the other two men, carrying their mugs, approached.

"Boys, this here is the man I was tellin' you about," Toombs said. "His name is Kilgore."

"Who are they?" Kilgore asked, taking in the two with a wave of his hand.

"This is Elvis Graves," Toombs said indicating the taller of the two. "And this here is Ramon Guerra."

Guerra had coal black hair, dark eyes, and a moustache that curled down around his mouth.

"You're a Mex," Kilgore said, stating the obvious.

"Si. Is that a problem, Senor?"

"If you can shoot a gun, I don't have no problem." Kilgore turned his attention to Graves.

"Whereabouts do you hale from, Graves?"

"Missouri."

"Missouri? Which side was you on? North or South?"

"Both."

"Both? How could you be on . . . oh, I get it. You was on whatever side was most handy at the time. Right?"

"Yeah."

"You don't talk much, do you?"

"No. I let my gun do the talking," Graves said.

"Can you vouch for 'im, Toombs?"

"Me 'n him's pulled a couple jobs together," Toombs said. "Weren't much, but Graves here, he didn't cause no trouble."

"How much money's in this?" Graves asked.

"It's hard to say," Kilgore said.

"I need money. Right now I ain't got two nickels to rub together, and I don't like it."

Kilgore smiled. "I like it when my partners are hungry. That's why I've got two plans. One to make walkin' around money fast, and one that'll take a little time, but the payoff will be bigger."

"A lot of money, good, Senor," Guerra said. "But a little money fast, is also good."

Kilgore smiled. "Toombs, I think these two boys are going to work out just fine."

Amon Kilgore led the men with him to a specific place on the Indianola Road.

"Toombs, you take Graves and get on that side of the road," Kilgore said. "Guerra, you stay here with me."

"How much money do you think the stage coach is carryin'?" Toombs asked.

"How much money you got?" Kilgore replied.

"I don't know. Two dollars, maybe."

"Then what do you care how much money the coach is carryin'?"

"There it is," Graves said, pointing.

Looking in the direction Graves indicated, they saw a cloud of dust billowing up from the road, and gleaming in the halo effect of the sun. The coach was too far away to see it as more than a black dot beneath the cloud, but it was approaching and would be here in just a few more minutes."

"I'll open the ball," Kilgore said. "Soon as I do, you boys join in."

Checking their pistols, the four men got into position, two men on either side of the road.

"I tell you the truth, Carl, I can't believe this is your last trip," the shotgun guard said. "Why you givin' up the job? They's no driver anywhere who can handle a six-horse team better'n you even if'n you are an old coot."

"Cause Miss Betty offered me a job tendin' bar over in Goliad. The work's easy, I can look at Miss Betty ever night, 'n I can drink all the beer I want."

"Ha, if you drink too much 'n wind up drunk, Miss Betty will be tossin' you out on your ass."

"Hell, Jordon, my quittin' ought to be good news for you," Carl replied. "Soon as I leave, they'll more 'n likely make you the driver."

"I don't want to drive," Jordan said.

"Why not? It pays more."

"Money ain't ever' thing. I like just sittin' up here, ridin' along, with nothin' to do but look at the rocks 'n the birds."

Carl laughed. "Don't ever say that to the boss man. You're supposed to be lookin' out for highway men."

"And I'm a doin' that," Jordan said. "But we ain't got that much money to speak of on this trip Nobody's gonna want what we got."

"Do you think a robber knows what we got on this stage? Of course not. He might be a thinkin' we're hauling a chest full of gold."

"No, no, they always know when we got a big shipment," Jordan said. "They's somebody always runs his mouth. Now that's when I'm on my toes, but this trip—it's nothin'."

There was a slight depression in the road and the coach dipped as it passed over it.

"Hmm, I'll bet the passengers got a thrill out of that," Jordan said.

"Warn't nothin' none of 'em ain't never done before," Carl said. "We only got Shuman, Bigelow, 'n Smith in the coach."

"All drummers," Jordan said. "Seein' as they're kind of competin' for the same dollars, it's a wonder that there don't no fights never break out when they're just a sittin' there dreamin'."

Kilgore looked around to make certain none of the others could be seen. By now the coach was less than a hundred yards away, and he could not only see it clearly, he could hear it; the clump of hoof beats, the rolling sound of the wheels, as well as the squeak and rattle of the coach as it rocked fore and aft on the through braces.

Kilgore waited until the coach was within twenty yards, then while still concealed, he shot the near-horse lead. The horse went down, and that stopped the coach.

"Here, what . . ." whatever question was going to be asked, was interrupted by a fusillade of gunfire. Both the driver and the guard were killed instantly, then Kilgore started shooting into the coach. The others followed his lead, and after several shots had been fired, Kilgore held up his hand.

The silence that followed the roar of guns seemed almost heavy, and Kilgore walked through the acrid smell of gun smoke, with pistol in hand, to look inside the bullet-riddled coach. There were three men, all dead, their bodies bloodied with wounds.

The robbery netted three hundred dollars from the money pouch, and another sixty-three dollars from the three passengers.

"Now," Kilgore said with a wide grin as he divided the money equally. "We got us enough money to move on to the big one."

LP Ranch, Jackson County, Texas:

The first man to sign up for the drive was Ian Campbell. This would be Campbell's third drive with Cade and Jeter, and though he was now 66 years old, he was still a good hand. Campbell, a Scotsman, had come to America when he was in his mid-twenties. Some said it was to find a better life, some said it was because he had been jilted by a woman, and a few even suggested that Ian, who even in his sixties was still a big and powerful man, had killed someone with his bare hands.

"Adams, Kingsley, Grant, Woodward, and Sullivan are gone," Colonel Puckett said. "You're going to have to come up with some new men from somewhere."

"Jeter, you ask around in Texana. I'm going back to Galveston; there are bound to be some men there who are looking for work," Cade said.

Cade took Arabella with him when he went back to Galveston. They still owned the lot where The Red House had been located, and he wasn't sure what she wanted to do with it. She had discussed rebuilding, and he was all for that, if that was her decision.

"Oh look," Arabella said, "they're rebuilding the Tremont."

"It's too bad it's not ready yet. We could spend the night there," Cade said with a prurient smile.

"I think not," Arabella said, lowering her lashes demurely.

"Well, we're not going home today," Cade said. "Where do you want to spend the night?"

"I'm thinking we should stay at the Bell and Sail. Didn't Virden invite us to stay there after the hurricane?"

"That's not what I had in mind, but that would be a good place to meet. I'm going to spend some time at the Saddle and Stirrup and see who I can round up for the drive."

"All right. I'm going to look for some new clothes for Magnolia and me."

The first person Cade saw when he entered the Saddle and Stirrup was Boo Rollins.

"Just the person I was hoping to run into," Cade said. "What are you drinking?"

Boo lifted his glass. "Beer—the best German beer on the island. What brings you back to town?"

"I'm looking to put together a crew to head north," Cade said as he indicated that he would have a beer as well.

"You don't say," Boo said. "Word was, most of the cattle drowned in the high water last fall. I didn't think there'd be a drive coming out of this part of the state."

Cade got his beer and sat down at the table. "They'll be at least one. Colonel Puckett's got the neighboring ranchers to agree to run what few cattle they have in one big herd."

"And you and Jeter are the contractors?"

"That's right. I'd like to gather up as many of the old hands as I can find. You, Finley, Macomb, Jenkins—anybody else who might be around."

"Finley's here in Galveston, but the other two—Macomb was kilt in the hurricane and nobody knows where Jenkins is. What about Ian Campbell? Have you run into him?"

"Yes, he wintered at the LP, and he's signed on to go," Cade said.

"I don't mean to be nosey, but who you got hired on to cook?"

Cade shook his head. "Jeter's in Texana now, trying to find a few new guys, and he's supposed to be scouting out a cook. With there being so few drives this year, we should be able to hire a good one."

"I'd hope so," Boo said. "That Weldon fellow was a sorry sack of shit."

Cade laughed. "I have to agree, but we were comparing him to Rufus Slade. There weren't many men who could put out the grub and run a chuck better than Rufus."

"Too bad that son-of-a-bitch had to kill him—when the drive was over, too. Rufus could have just rode out of Abilene and nobody would'a knowed who or what he was," Boo said.

"He was a good man."

"That he was. When do you plan to start?"

"I'd like you to get to the LP as soon as you can, because when we left, the ranchers had already started the gather. They're putting them up in Puckett's pasture on the Crooked Creek."

"I can do that."

"Good. I'll find out if Art Finley can go with us, and maybe I can find a couple of others," Cade said.

"All right. Where should we meet up with you?"

A sheepish grin crossed Cade's face. "At the Bell and Sail."

"What? A cattleman on the wharf? That's a bad sign. Somethin's not gonna go right," Boo said as he drained the last of his mug.

Arabella was pleased to be back in Galveston. It had been a little over six months since the hurricane, and most of the business seemed to be open or in the process of rebuilding. She went first to the site where The Red House had stood. The lot, with the exception of the tree where the wagon had snagged, was swept clean.

She walked over the ground, in her mind laying out the design for the new building. The house would be raised to at least seventeen feet allowing water to flow beneath it. That would protect her carpets when another storm came.

She smiled. Her carpets. They had been so important to her, and yet this was the first time she had even thought about them.

She had told Cade she would be shopping for clothes for her and Magnolia, but instead she went first to the Hutchings Sealy National Bank.

"Miss Dupree," Benton Caldwell said as he took her hand, lifting it to his lips. "I wasn't sure what had happened to you after the storm. Did you return to New Orleans?"

Arabella flinched. Caldwell was one of the few Galvestonians who had been a customer at Lafitte's Blacksmith Shop Bar.

"I did not," Arabella said raising her head in a defiant gesture.

"Oh, my dear, I did not intend to offend you," the loan officer said. "It's just that you were so good at what you did, I thought you might enjoy returning to that line of work."

"Mr. Caldwell, I came to the HSNB this morning with the intention of borrowing money to rebuild my establishment—a boarding house, a legitimate boarding house that served this city well. I thank you for your time." She rose from the chair and without another word left Caldwell's office.

When she reached the street, she clinched her teeth in an attempt to hold back tears, but she was not successful. Her words to Magnolia saying that you can't un ring a bell were never more true. The tears streaming down her cheeks were tears of rage and tears of regret. They were also for the realization that The Red House was as much a part of her past as her employment at Lafitte's Blacksmith Shop Bar.

8

Jeter Willis tied his horse off in front of the Ace High Saloon in Refugio, Texas. He had come to find a few more drovers for the upcoming drive.

"What's goin' on?" he asked when he approached a group of men gathering in the street.

"You see that hat lyin' in the middle of the street there?" a man replied.

Looking in the direction indicated, Jeter saw the low-crown hat the man had spoken of.

"I see it."

"Well, that feller over there has a bet with that boy down at the far end of the street." He pointed to a large man with a cannon-ball like head that set directly on broad shoulders. "The kid says he can scoop up that hat when his horse is at full gallop."

"How much is the bet?"

"Five dollars."

"All right boy!" the big man shouted. "You goin' to make us wait all day?"

"Don't rush the boy, Penrod," another said. "Give 'im time to get hisself ready."

From the opposite end of the street the young man urged his horse into a gallop. As he approached the hat, he leaned down so far from the saddle that he had to hold himself on by hooking his foot on the saddle horn. With the horse at a full gallop, its hooves kicking up chunks of dirt behind, the boy grabbed the hat, then swung back up into the saddle. He let the horse slow then came back with a big smile on his face, holding the hat out in front of him.

"Here's your hat, Mister," he said.

"Penrod grabbed the two five dollar bills from the man who had been holding the bet.

"You lost the bet, sonny," he said.

"Penrod, what are you talking about?" one of those who had been watching, shouted in anger. "The boy scooped up the hat just like he said he would. You lost that bet 'n the money belongs to the boy."

"No it don't neither," Penrod said. "The bet was, he could grab the hat at a full gallop while he was still sittin' in the saddle. It's clear he wasn't sittin' in the saddle."

"Huh, uh, that ain't what I said," the boy protested. "I said without leavin' the saddle."

"Yeah, well, you done that. You left the saddle."

"Mister, I watched the boy same as ever' one else did," Jeter said. "He had one foot in the stirrup and the other foot hooked over the saddle horn. The saddle horn and the stirrup, are both part of the saddle. That means he never left the saddle."

"Yeah, that's true," another said. "You owe the boy five dollars."

"I tell you what. I'll give you a chance to make some real money," Penrod said to the boy. "I'll put a handkerchief on the street, 'n I'll bet you twenty dollars you can't pick it up like you done the hat."

"I ain't got twenty dollars," the boy said.

"Too bad. You ain't got this five dollars neither, 'cause far as I'm concerned, you lost the bet."

"I'll lend the boy twenty dollars," Jeter said. "You give him back the five dollars he put up, and we'll forget about the first bet."

"How do I know you got twenty dollars? A stranger just ridin' in here. You look like you don't even have the price of a drink," Penrod replied.

"I've got the money," he said. "Are you up for the bet? Or were you just runnin' your mouth?"

"Mister, nobody talks to me like that," Penrod said, angrily.

"I just did. Now are you goin' to bet, or not?"

"You're willin' to put up twenty dollars just to see that boy scoop up a handkerchief from the street?"

"Yes."

"Mister," the boy said. "I don't know you. I don't want to take a chance on losin' your money."

"My name's Jeter, Jeter Willis. And what's your name?"

"Jones. George Washington Jones, but most folks just call me GW."

"All right, GW. Now tell me, do you think you can pick up the handkerchief, same way you did the hat?"

"Yes, sir, I'm pretty sure I can do it. But what if I can't? Then you'd lose your money."

"You let me worry about that, GW. If you think you can do it, I'm willin' to back you."

GW smiled. "I can do it."

"Good," Jeter said. "Now, Penrod, I think I heard you called. First thing I want from you is the five dollars you took from the boy. The second thing I want is for you to put your twenty dollars right here, under this rock." Jeter put a twenty-dollar bill on the boardwalk, then picked up a rock from the street.

"And the third thing is a clear understandin' of the rules. The bet is, this boy, GW, can scoop up a handkerchief from the middle of the street without leaving the saddle. And that means any part of the saddle."

"All right," Penrod said as he put his money under the rock. "Let's see what he can do." He pulled a handkerchief from his pocket and dropped it in the center of the street.

By now the little group of ten or twelve, who had watched the first bet, had grown to a small crowd.

GW smiled at Jeter and dipped his head. He rode to the far end of the street, and then turned his horse. For a moment he just sat there.

"He's a thinkin' he can't do it," a man said. "He's gonna chicken out."

Then all at once the horse exploded in a full gallop as horse and rider barreled down the street. There was a gasp when GW disappeared from the saddle and some thought he had fallen off. Jeter saw exactly what he had done, and was amazed with the boy's agility.

GW had swung his leg over the saddle and was now riding with one foot in the stirrup and the other stretched out behind him. He was hanging on to the cantle with one hand, while the other hand was but an inch above the ground. He scooped up the handkerchief, then without remounting, brought the horse around, and back, where he stepped down onto the ground.

Those who had gathered to watch the performance applauded.

Jeter saw the way GW was holding the handkerchief, and he went over to retrieve it.

"Mr. Willis . . ." GW said.

"I've got it, GW," Jeter said, smiling at the boy. He reached down to take the handkerchief, from the top, holding it the same way GW had been holding it. He saw what many others had not yet noticed. When Penrod had put the handkerchief down, he put it over a horse apple.

Jeter walked over to Penrod. "I believe this belongs to you," he said, shoving the handkerchief turd into Penrod's hand.

"What the hell?" Penrod shouted, angrily, dropping the handkerchief on the ground, which left him holding a palm full of shit.

The others laughed.

Jeter picked up the two twenty-dollar bills, pocketed one, and gave the other to GW.

"Tell me, son, do you have a job?" Jeter asked.

"No, sir, not really. Mostly I just do odd jobs and such as I can get."

"How would you like to make a trail drive to Kansas?"

The smile on GW's face grew even broader. "Yes, sir, I'd love to do that!"

"You're hired," Jeter said.

When Cade and Arabella got back from Galveston, he was pleased to find that Jeter had come up with enough men to round out the crew.

"It's good that so many of our old drovers are going up with us again," Jeter said.

"Yeah, I like to know my men," Cade said. "Is there anybody who caught your attention—anybody who might be a troublemaker?"

"I don't think so. But there's one kid that's gonna be good for entertainment," Jeter said as he proceeded to tell about how he had met GW Jones. "Oh, by the way, who'd you get for the cookie?" Cade asked.

"Me? I thought that was your job?"

"I hired Ike Weldon last year and ever' body grumbled the whole trip. I think it's your turn to hunt one down," Jeter said. "But you'd better do it right quick, cause seven of the men are already in Mr. Puckett's bunkhouse raring to get on the trail."

"I'll be out on the hustings first thing in the morning."

Cade rode out before sunrise, going to every community in Jackson and Matagorda Counties. The cook was without

76

doubt the most important position to fill, and he had hoped Jeter would have been successful. Rufus Slade had been the cook on Cade's first drive up to Abilene, and he had taught Cade a lot—where the best bedding grounds were, where the best crossings were, where to get the best price for supplies, and even what bars to visit along the way.

As it turned out, Rufus had been a man with a past. Ruthless, as he was known then, had been a gunfighter who roamed the Southwest. When the cattle drive reached Abilene, they found the town was dominated by an evil despot, who used a gunfighter by the name of Enos Crites as his enforcer. At one time Rufus and Crites had been cohorts, having ridden the outlaw trail together. Now, in Abilene, they found themselves on opposite sides, and circumstances caused the two men to meet, face to face in the middle of Texas Street.

"We had some good times together," Crites said.

"Yes, we did."

"But I always knew I was better than you."

Rufus turned in such a way as to present himself to Crites in profile. "Prove it," he said.

Crites pulled his pistol so fast that Cade couldn't even follow it. There was a jerk of his shoulder and the gun was in his hand. Cade's eyes had been on Crites, rather than Rufus, so he missed the fact that Rufus's draw had been even faster. Rufus fired first.

Crites caught the ball high in his chest. He fired his own gun then, but it was just a convulsive action and the bullet went into the dirt just before he dropped his gun and slapped his hand over the wound. He looked down in surprise as blood streamed through his fingers, turning his shirt bright red. He took two staggering steps toward Rufus, then fell to his knees. He looked up at Rufus.

"How'd you do that?" he asked in surprise. "How'd you get your gun out that fast?" He smiled, then coughed, and

flecks of blood came from his mouth. He breathed hard a couple of times. "I was sure I was faster than you."

"Looks like you were wrong," Rufus said easily.

After defeating the best that the despot had to offer, it appeared as if the battle had been won. But a cowardly rifleman, hidden on the roof behind the false front of the saloon, killed Rufus from afar.

Cade went on to win the ultimate battle, but at the loss of a friend, and the best cook who had ever taken a chuck wagon up the trail.

By comparison, last year's cook, Ike Weldon, came up woefully short, and Cade was determined to find a cook that would meet the expectations of the men.

Remigio Vasquez was his first choice. Vasquez was the cook for the Lazy L Ranch, and his wagon was always one of the most popular during the gathering when all the herds were separated in the spring. At first, Cade had thought the hot peppers and chili powder were a little overpowering, but the men couldn't get enough of it. If he could hire Remigio away from the Lazy L, he wouldn't have to look any further.

Vasquez, who was in his sixties, was bald, with a gray beard. He was rolling out dough for biscuits as Cade was talking to him.

"I appreciate the offer, Mr. McCall, and the money sounds good," Vasquez said. "But I'm just real comfortable here. Mr. Lyman's a good man to work for, and to tell the truth, I just don't know if I'm up to makin' another cattle drive. They're awful tirin', 'n my bones is gettin' awful old."

"I understand," Cade said. "I came to you because you were very highly recommended by some of the men who had made drives with you."

"I'm just real pleased that they appreciated me," Vasquez said. "You might try Max Rand. I broke him in some years ago, 'n he took to cookin' just real good. Don't know if you can hire him away, though, seein' as how he took hisself a real good job cookin' for the cafe over in Matagorda."

When Cade found Rand, he wasn't interested in the job. He made three more attempts to find someone, but no one was interested.

That left two possibilities: either one of the cowboys would take over the wagon, or he would look up Ike Weldon. Inquiring about Weldon, Cade was told he would find him cooking in a saloon in Bacliff, a town about fifteen miles from Galveston.

"Yeah," Weldon said, when Cade confronted him. "I heard they was a drive bein' put together. So, you're a' wantin' me to cook for you again this year are you?"

"I do need a cook," Cade replied, dodging the issue of whether or not he actually 'wanted' Weldon.

"I hear tell you been askin' aroun' tryin' to find someone else. How come you didn't come to me first?"

"I heard that you had a job, and I wasn't sure you'd be interested."

The discussion between Cade and Weldon was taking place in the kitchen of the Six-Shooter Saloon which, in addition to serving drinks, had a limited menu.

"Yeah, well, I ain't got a job no more," Weldon said as he took off his apron and lay it on the cutting table. Even as he did so, there were two strips of bacon, twitching in a pan on the stove. "When do I start?"

"Aren't you going to finish the meal you're cooking?" Cade asked.

"It ain't my problem," Weldon said. "Like I just told you, I don't work here no more."

"I have to tell you, Weldon, that's not the kind of attitude I like in someone who's working for me. I value loyalty."

"I ain't bein' disloyal to you, I'm bein' disloyal to Arnie Frank. He's the one that owns this place, 'n to tell the truth, I never liked that son of a bitch anyway."

"You don't understand. When I'm talking about loyalty, I'm talking about loyalty to your obligation," Cade said.

"I was loyal to you last year, wasn't I? Hell, you should like it that I'm more loyal to you than I am to Arnie. Besides which, where you goin' to get yourself another trail cook? Nowhere, that's where. If you could'a got one, you'd 'a already had one 'n you wouldn' a' come to me."

Cade didn't respond right away. He knew that Weldon was right; there was no other trail cook available.

"All right. Get out to the LP and start puttin' your wagon together. I want to head out by the end of the week."

LP Ranch:

It was now time for Kilgore to put together the second of his money-grabbing schemes. The stage robbery had filled his immediate needs but he wanted more. It was his intention to assemble an outfit to take a combined herd up to Abilene. But, as before, when he had taken the Rocking D herd, only about half the cows would actually make it all the way to the rail head. Kilgore smiled as he contemplated the plan. It was much safer to take cows this way than to risk getting killed by cattle rustling.

When Amon Kilgore knocked on the front door of the "big house" at the LP ranch, it was answered by a Mexican woman.

"May I help you, Senor?"

"Yeah, I wanna see Puckett."

"And who are you, Senor?"

"The name is Kilgore. Amon Kilgore." Kilgore tried to step into the house, but the woman stopped him.

"Wait here, Senor, I will find Senor Puckett."

"What do you mean wait here? I ain't goin' to just stand here 'cause some Mex told me to."

"Please, Senor, wait here."

Kilgore nodded. "All right," he said. "Seein' as you asked me real nice, I reckon I can stay here."

As Kilgore waited, he stepped out to the edge of the porch to take in the ranch. Colonel Puckett was a very wealthy man, and his ranch was an obvious display of his wealth. One day, if things worked out well for him, he, Amon Kilgore, would have a ranch just as nice as this one.

"Senor Kilgore, Colonel Puckett will see you now," the woman said when she returned to the porch.

Kilgore was led through the well-appointed great room, and into a smaller room. Kilgore was impressed that a man could be so rich as to have an extra room in his house that wasn't used for anything but an office.

Puckett was sitting behind his desk, and without rising, he made a motion toward a chair that sat across from the desk. In one corner of the office, Kilgore noticed, there was a small seating area, with two leather chairs. There, too, was a silver coffee service and he could smell the coffee, but none was offered.

"What can I do for you, Kilgore?" Puckett asked.

"I read in the paper that all the cattlemen are combining their stock for the drive this year," Kilgore said.

"Yes, since we all lost so many cows in the storm, that's what we've decided to do."

Kilgore smiled, and nodded. "Yes, sir, I've been sayin' that same thing, tellin' anyone who'd listen, that the best thing for all the cattlemen would be to combine the herds."

"Well, I'm glad that you agree," Puckett replied. So far Puckett had shown only the most cursory interest in the reason for Kilgore's visit.

"Yes, sir, well, here's the thing. I got me a real good outfit put together, 'n what I'd like to do is be your trail boss."

"You're saying you want to contract your services to take the cattle to Abilene?" Puckett asked.

"Yes, sir, 'n seein' as I heard they'd all be combinin' their herds with yours, well, I figure you're the one that'll be makin' the decision as to who will be doin' it for you."

81

"If you read the story in the paper, then you also read that I've already made my decision," Puckett said. "I'll be going with McCall and Willis."

"I know that's what the paper said, only, you ain't left yet, so it ain't too late for you to change your mind."

"Kilgore, last year you took a herd up for John Dennis, didn't you?"

"Yes, sir, I did."

"And from what I understand, you lost so many cattle en-route that John barely broke even on the year."

"Yes, sir, but you can't be a' blamin' me for all that. They was a lot of things that just happened, is all."

"That may be so, but those things didn't 'just happen' with McCall and Willis. Those two men got nearly all my cows through, and in time to make the best deal possible."

"Yeah, but here's the thing," Kilgore said with a conspiratorial grin. "Iffen you'd go with me, I'd charge you a dollar less per head, 'n you wouldn' have to tell none o' the other owners. You could just let 'em think it was still four dollars a head that it was costin' 'em, 'n you could pocket the difference."

"Thank you for your offer, Mr. Kilgore," Puckett replied, stiffly. "But I would not be interested in cheating my fellow cattlemen. I'll go with McCall and Willis. I'll have Fernanda escort you out."

9

Texana:

Jeter was at the blacksmith shop when he saw GW Jones and two others riding into town. He stepped out into the street to flag them down.

"You lookin' for me, GW?" he asked.

"Yes, sir, what I was wantin' to know is if you'd have room for two more hands," GW said. "This here's Timmy Ponder and he's Troy Hastings."

Neither of the two looked as old as GW.

"How old are you two boys?" Jeter asked.

"Does it matter how old we are if we can do the work?" one of the two asked.

"Which one are you?"

"I'm Troy Hastings."

"Well, Troy, no, it doesn't matter."

"They're both good boy . . . uh . . . men," JW said. "I've worked with both of 'em before."

"What kind of work did you do?"

"Me 'n GW loaded 'n unloaded freight wagons," Hastings said. "Timmy, he took care of the horses 'n mules."

"Why'd you quit? Or were you fired?"

"Wasn't neither one," GW said. "Mr. Matthews only hired us when he needed us, 'n he said we did real good while we was workin' for 'im. You can ask 'im."

"I may do that," Jeter said.

"Uh . . ." Hastings started to say, and he looked at the other two before he went any further.

"You may as well tell 'im, Troy, he's liable to find out some other way, then it'll be even worse," GW said.

"What is it you need to tell me?"

"I kilt a feller," Hastings said.

"What?"

"My ma 'n pa is both dead, 'n I was livin' with my sister. She was about six year's older 'n me. Anyhow I was just comin' back from choppin' some wood' 'n I heard her a screamin' 'n such. When I run into the house, I seen a man cut her throat with a knife he was holdin'. I still had the axe in my hand so what I done was...I chopped his head open. I kilt 'im right there."

"What about your sister?"

"She died. She tried to say somethin' to me....I could see her mouth movin', but she wasn't makin' no sound."

"The sheriff, he didn't make no charges or nothin'," GW pointed out.

"I would think not," Jeter said. "If ever there was just cause for a killin', that would be it."

"I just wish I'd got there a minute quicker 'n I could 'a kept 'im from killin' Lily like he done."

"I'm sure you do, son," Jeter said, clasping his hand on the boy's shoulder. "You've got a job with me."

"Thank you, sir."

"Now, you men get your business done, and then ride on over to the LP," Jeter said, purposely using the word, *men.* "Tell Colonel Puckett you're hired on with McCall and

Willis. He'll put you up in the bunkhouse and provide you with board and found until we move out."

Huge smiles spread across their faces.

"I promise you, Mr. Willis, you won't be sorry," GW said.

When Cade returned to Texana, he saw Jeter's horse tied up in front of the hardware store, so he went in to find him.

"I thought a new axe and saw might come in handy," Jeter said by way of greeting.

"Good idea."

"How'd you do?" Jeter did not specifically ask about the cook.

"Get your tools, and then come meet me at the Horn Toad."

Cade was studying a piece of paper when Jeter got to the saloon. He grabbed a glass of beer and sat down.

"We can count on Ian Campbell, Boo Rollins, Art Finley, Muley Morris, and Petey Malone."

"That's good," Jeter said. "Everyone of 'em rode with us last year. Anybody else?"

"Yeah, I signed on a new man, Jeremiah Mudd. Nobody knows much about him, but he says he made a couple of drives out of Wyoming before he came here. Now, what about you?"

"I got Mo Bender," Jeter said as he took a swallow of beer. "He rode for Chris Dumey last year, and since Dumey'll have some cows in the herd, Mo should be a pretty good hand. And the kid brought me two more, Timmy Ponder and Troy Hastings. They aren't any older than GW is, but I was only fourteen myself when I started out, back before the war."

Cade added Jeter's names to his list. "Sounds like we're done."

"I don't think so," Jeter said.

"Jeter, we've signed up ten men and including the two of us, that's twelve men. If we can't take 2500 cows up the trail, I think we'd better get out of the business."

"Aren't you forgettin' someone?" Jeter asked.

Cade looked over his paper. He shook his head. "No, I think I've got 'em all."

"The cook? Who'd you get for the cook?"

"I went to see Remigio Vasquez," Cade said.

"And?"

"He says he's too old, but he recommended a couple others."

"And?"

"They don't want to go."

"So what you're telling me is, we're stuck with Weldon," Jeter said.

"Was he really that bad? Maybe we can convince him to put in some of Remigio's peppers."

"Remigio's peppers are not going to help Ike Weldon's cooking." Jeter drained the last of his beer and stood up. "One good thing, we don't have to eat it tonight. What do you think Maggie will have for supper?"

"It's dinner."

"It's too late for dinner," Jeter said. "It's supper time."

Cade shook his head. "You've not been listening. Both Arabella and Maggie insist that supper is dinner."

"Well if that's the case, what do they call dinner?"

"They call it lunch."

"Lunch? Nah, lunch is somethin' you keep in your saddle bag, when you don't have time for anything else," Jeter insisted.

Cade chuckled as he grabbed his hat and started for the door. "You just wait, you'll come around."

"Hey, Cade, look at that," Jeter said, looking through the window as they passed by the Buckner-Ragsdale Mercantile store. He was pointing to a silver brush and comb set. "Now, isn't that just about the prettiest thing you ever did see?"

"Turned into a dandy, have you?" Cade asked with a teasing little laugh.

Jeter scowled. "Not for me, you numskull. I mean for Maggie. You think she'd like somethin' like that?"

"She probably would, but you know what you're doing, don't you?" Cade asked.

"What's that?"

"Well, if you buy something for Maggie, that means I'll have to buy something for Arabella."

"Well, don't you want to?"

"Yeah," Cade said with a smile. "I do want to."

Horn Toad Saloon, Texana

Kilgore was sitting at a table with Bull Kolinsky. Bull stood, three inches over six feet tall and weighed well over two hundred pounds. None of it was fat. He had a short forehead, a prominent eyebrow ridge, gray, beady eyes, flattened nose, a protruding lower lip, and a receding chin. His job was that of a wagonwright at the blacksmith shop. He was very strong and often, when changing a wheel, disdained the use of a jack, holding the wagon bed up with his bare hands while someone else fitted on the wheel.

"You know what I want you to do, don't you?" Kilgore said.

"Yeah, you want me to pick a fight with this McCall fella," Bull replied, in a low, rumbling voice.

"Don't talk so loud," Kilgore cautioned.

"This here's the only way I know how to talk," Bull replied.

"Well keep it a little quieter," Kilgore said as he leaned closer to Bull. "You understand I want more than a fight. I want him hurt. Do you think you can do that?"

"I can kill 'im if you want me to."

"No, no, you don't have to go that far—maybe a broken arm, or better yet, a broken leg."

"What'd this McCall do to you? Why do you want 'im hurt?" Bull asked.

"I want him hurt so's he can't go on this cattle drive Puckett's got lined up. You think you can do that for me?"

"How much you payin'?"

"Fifty dollars."

Bull held out his hand. "Give me the money."

"Nope," Kilgore said. "After the jobs done."

"Then find somebody else." Bull stood quickly.

"Hold on." Kilgore took out a ten dollar bill and handed it over. "This is a hell of a lot of money. I'm trustin' you'll get the job done."

"Has Big Bull ever let you down?"

MW Ranch:

Over the supper table that evening Cade and Jeter compared notes about the men they had gotten for the upcoming cattle drive.

"I figure we'll put Rollins on point," Cade said.

"Yeah and two of the young'uns, I'd say Hastings and Jones will ride drag," Jeter said.

"They're going to be eating a lot of dust," Cade said. "You think they can handle that?"

Jeter laughed. "That's what young'uns do on cattle drives. Hell, my first two or three drives, I swallowed enough dirt to start my own ranch."

"How long do you think you'll be gone?" Arabella asked.

"It could be another three months," Cade said.

"That's a very long time."

"No longer than it was last year."

"*Oui*, but when you made the drive last year, I had *Maison Rouge*, and all the people who lived there to keep me company. Here, I have nothing to do while you're gone."

"We won't be gone as long as we were gone last winter, and besides you and Maggie have each other," Cade said. "And there's Titus and Mary. They'll be putting in a garden before long and you'll want to help them."

"All that is true. We did get along just fine, but, Cade . . . ." Arabella stopped in mid sentence.

"What is it? What's wrong?" Cade asked.

"It's just that . . . it's just that I miss you so much."

A broad smile crossed Cade's face. "And I miss you, too, but when we get back it'll be that much better."

"You know what I'm thinkin'?" Jeter asked. "I mean, seein' as how these two fixed us this real good tastin' supper and all, I'm thinkin' that this might be a good time to give you a little present I bought." Jeter directed his smile toward Maggie

"*Pour moi*? For me?" Maggie said, translating quickly.

"Yeah, for you. I tell you what," Jeter said with a little laugh. "If I stay around you long enough, I'm goin' to have to learn French, I can see that right now."

"*Je serai très heureux de vous enseigner, Monsieur Jeter,*" Maggie said in a low, throaty voice. When she spoke the name 'Jeter', it came out as 'Zheeter'.

"Whoa now, I don't have any idea what you just said, but I sure did like listenin' to you say it."

Arabella laughed, the laughter sounding like the tinkling of wind chimes. "She said she would be very happy to teach you, Mister Jeter."

Jeter walked over to the saddlebags he had brought into the cabin with him, and pulled out the silver comb and brush set.

"I thought you might like this," he said.

"Oh, thank you, Jeter, it is beautiful!" Maggie said effusively, augmenting her thanks with a kiss.

"Now, see there, Cade. If you had somethin' for Arabella, why, she might've givin' you a kiss too," Jeter said. "Oh, wait, you did get somethin' for her, didn't you?"

"You have something for me?"

Cade went over to his saddlebags and withdrew a small, black-cloth bag. Returning to the table he gave the little bag to Arabella. Smiling she pulled the drawstring then turned it up to drop the contents in her hand. It was a gold ring, and she looked up at Cade with a shocked expression on her face.

"Cade, this . . ."

"Yes it is," Cade said. "It's a wedding ring. I think you aren't supposed to wear it until we're married."

"You are asking me to marry you?"

"I am, I mean, that's why I bought the ring. And if you say no right now, in front of Jeter and Maggie, well I have to tell you, it's goin' to be damn embarrassing."

A huge smile spread across Arabella's face. "What makes you think I would say no? Of course, I'll marry you, Cade McCall." She threw her arms around him as he hugged her too him.

"We'll get married this summer as soon as we get back from Abilene."

"That makes me very happy," Arabella said. "Now I know what Magnolia and I will be doing this summer."

"And what is that?"

"We'll be learning to sew. My first project will be my wedding dress."

10

Horn Toad Saloon, Texana:

Boo Rollins asked Cade to meet him at the Horn Toad, and as soon as Cade stepped inside, he saw Rollins and two other men sitting at a table.

"Cade, I want you to meet a couple of fellers I ran into," Rollins said. "This here's Alberto Tangora, and this is Esteban Garcia."

Cade extended his hand to each of the men as he nodded his head.

"If we've got a spot for them, I think they'd make us some mighty fine hands," Boo said.

"We could use a couple more men, especially since we've got some youngsters with us," Cade said. "Have either of you made a drive before?"

"*Si, Senor*, we both made many trips with *Senor* Goodnight," Tangora said. "Estaban even made the first drive when Senor Loving got his cows to the Mescaleros."

"That was to Fort Sumner wasn't it?" Cade asked.

"Si, Senor," Garcia said. "We call it *Bosque Redondo*."

"Well, it's the lore of any roundup what you men had to go through to get to the tribe," Cade said. "People say the cows went three days without water."

"That's true, but along the Pecos—the *serpiente de cascabel*—that's what I remember most."

Cade chuckled, recognizing the Spanish word.

"Well I can't promise you we won't run into any rattlesnakes, but if you men can make it on the Goodnight Trail, you can ride with McCall and Willis all the way to Abilene," Cade said. "Boo, good job, finding these two; take them out to the LP and . . ."

"McCall, get them whiffy Mexican sons of bitches out of here! They're stinking up the whole place," someone shouted his loud, booming voice, bringing all other conversation to a complete stop.

"Bull, there's no need to call 'em out," the bartender said. "Nobody's causing any trouble."

"Well, what do you call this stink? That's causin' me trouble. I can't taste my beer, the stink's so bad," Bull Kolinsky said. "I say I don't want these Mexicans in here, 'n if McCall don't take 'em out of here now, I'm goin' to throw both of 'em out, 'n then I'm goin' to whip McCall's ass."

"Tell me, Mr.Kolinsky, just how is it that I've offended you?" Cade asked.

"You brung them two Mexicans in here, that's what you done that offended me."

"Well, not to make a point of it, but these two gentlemen were already here when I came into the saloon," Cade said. "The smell didn't bother you then so why are you bothered by it now?"

Bull ran his hand through his hair as he tried to come up with a response to Cade.

"It's you that bothers me," he finally said. "You think you're better 'n ever' one, but you ain't," Bull said.

"Oh, I'm not better than *every*one, Bull." Cade flashed a cynical smile. "Just some people."

Bull was uncertain as to whether or not he had been insulted, and he blinked several times, then raised his arm and pointed a thick finger at Cade.

"Like I said, I'm goin' to beat the hell out of you."

Cade walked over to the bar.

"Mr. Kolinsky, you and I have obviously gotten off on the wrong foot this morning." He turned to the bartender who, like everyone else in the saloon was watching the drama being played out in front of them. Cade put a dime down on the bar. "I'll have a beer, Samson, and draw one for my friend, too."

Samson drew a beer and set the mug in front of Cade. He drew a second mug of beer and put it in front of Bull, who with an angry swipe of his hand, sent it onto the floor, spewing the golden liquid.

"I know what you're a doin' and you ain't gonna fool old Bull. You're a shakin' in your boots, cause you know what's a comin'."

Cade lifted the beer and took a swallow before he replied. "All right, Mr. Kolinsky, you go ahead and do what you feel you have to do."

"Huh?"

Cade smiled. "Beat the hell out of me," he said.

This wasn't the kind of reaction Bull was used to getting, and for just a moment, he had a confused look on his face. Then the expression turned to one of anger, and with a roar, he lowered his head and charged Cade, depending on his strength and size to overwhelm his opponent.

Cade, still holding his beer mug in his right hand, stepped to one side and with the fingers of his left hand extended and joined, he made a hard thrust into Bull's solar plexus. That had the effect of taking all the wind out of the big man and he bent over, as he tried to catch his breath. While he was vulnerable, Cade brought his heavy beer mug crashing down over Bull's head. He crashed to the floor, with his head striking the brass railing at the foot the bar.

"Son of a bitch!" one of the saloon patrons said, the words spoken not in anger, but in awe. "I never thought I'd see anyone whup Bull like that."

"He didn't whup 'im, he tricked 'im," another said.

"You mean, by knocking him out, he tricked him?"

"No, I mean . . . no, hell, you're right. He did whup 'im."

Cade lifted the mug to take a swallow of beer, then saw that the glass was empty, the beer having all splashed out when he brought it down on Bull's head. He held it out toward the barkeep who, like everyone else, was stunned at how quickly, and how easily, Cade McCall had handled the big man.

"Samson, it looks like I'm going to have to have a refill," Cade said. "The beer seems to have splashed out."

Cade put a nickel on the bar, but the bartender pushed it back.

"No, sir, Mr. McCall, this is on the house," Samson said.

"No it ain't," Boo Rollins said. He smiled. "I aim to pay for it. It was damn fine, watchin' ole Bull get took down like that."

With a groan, Bull began stirring, then with some effort, managed to regain his feet.

"What happened?" he asked. His left eye was swollen and black, though the bruise covered more than his eye. It also spilled down to his cheekbone.

"You tripped and fell," Cade said. "And you hit the foot rail. Look at yourself in the mirror."

Bull did so, touching the bruise gently, with the tips of his fingers. "Damn!" he said. "The foot rail did that?"

"It sure did."

Bull put his fingers to the top of his head, then winced with they encountered the bump there.

"What I don't understand is how come the top of my head hurts," Bull questioned in sincere confusion.

"I don't know, you must've bumped it on the bar when you fell," Cade said.

"Yeah, I must've done that." The confusion on Bull's face became even more pronounced, and he pointed a thick finger at Cade. "Say, wasn't me 'n you . . .?"

"Having a drink together?" Cade said, answering Bull's unfinished question. "Yes we were, but you seem to have spilled yours in the fall. Samson, give this man another beer; it's on me."

"Yes, sir, coming right up," the bartender said, and it was no quicker said than done, because a large mug of beer appeared on the bar in front of Bull.

"Thanks," Bull said, lifting the mug.

Leaving the saloon, Cade rode with Rollins, Tangora, and Garcia out to the LP Ranch, to introduce his two new riders.

"So, I hear you had a run-in with Bull Kolinsky," Puckett said.

"What? How could you possibly know that? It just happened."

"Art Finley saw it, and he rode out here to tell me about it."

"Hmm. I didn't notice Art in the saloon."

Puckett chuckled. "Understandable, you were a little busy at the time."

"I don't know what set him off," Cade said. "He said it was because of Alberto and Estaban, but they were already in the bar, so I don't think that was it."

"Men like that don't need anything to set them off," Puckett said. "He's a big strong man who enjoys beating people up. I expect he was very surprised when he came to and learned you had whipped him."

Cade laughed. "He won't know unless someone tells him. He couldn't remember a thing."

"Oh, you can be sure there've been plenty of people who've enjoyed telling him all about it," Puckett said, "which means he might have it in for you."

"You're probably right."

"So, all I can say is you keep an eye open for him."

"I will," Cade promised.

"Now what about the company, have you got it assembled?" Puckett asked.

"Yes, sir. All we have left is the final gather, and as soon as the other ranchers get their cows collected, we'll be ready to go."

"That's good," Puckett said. "You know some of the others are questioning your fees. They swear you and Jeter are going to make as much if not more than they are from this drive."

"And what do you say, Mr. Puckett?"

"I'm not complaining. It's a good comfortable feeling staying at home, and knowing that my cows are in good hands. I'm glad to have McCall and Willis in charge."

"Thank you, sir. We'll try our best to earn your trust."

When Amon Kilgore walked down to the freight wagon yard, he saw Bull Kolinsky walking across the lot with a huge wagon wheel under each arm.

"I thought you said you could handle 'im," Kilgore said.

"What ya talkin' about?"

Your fight with McCall. If you can call it a fight."

Bull nodded his head. "Some of the ones in the Horn Toad told me I was in a fight, but I don't remember nothin' about it. It's like one minute I was just standin' there at the bar, 'n the next minute I was wakin' up on the floor. I don't remember nothin' in between, 'n wouldn't have no idea there'd even been a fight, 'ceptin' for people tellin' me about it."

"Does that mean you also forgot about the fifty dollars I paid you?"

"Fifty dollars?"

"Yeah, I gave you fifty dollars to make it so McCall couldn't make the drive. Are you telling me you don't remember that, either?"

"Wait a minute, I do sort of remember talking to you about somethin' like that."

"Well, you didn't get the job done, so I guess I'm just out my fifty dollars," Kilgore said.

"No, you ain't out," Bull said. "If I took the money from you to do somethin', 'n I didn't do it, I'll give you back your money."

Bull put his hand in his pocket and pulled out a ten-dollar bill.

"Where's the rest of it?" Kilgore asked.

"I . . . I don't know. I must've spent it, or lost it, I don't know what happened."

"So, what you're sayin' is, you beat me out of forty dollars."

"No, wait here. I'll get the money from the boss. He'll loan it to me."

Fifteen minutes later Kilgore, with a smile spread across his face, left the freight yard forty dollars richer. He took a risk, cheating Bull out of the money like that; Bull could break him into little pieces if he wanted to. On the other hand, Bull wasn't very smart and Kilgore was certain he would always be able to outwit him.

11

LP Ranch:

"All right, men," Cade said, addressing the cowboys when all were assembled for the first time. "The McCall and Willis Cattle Company for the Combined Herd Drive of 1870 will get underway as soon as the last of the cattle get the road brand."

"Men?" Mudd said with a snicker. "We got at least three boys here, who's still wet behind their ears." A few of the other cowboys laughed, while Ponder, Hastings, and Jones, the three youngest, flushed in embarrassment.

"Mr. Mudd, if Mr. Ponder, Mr. Hastings, and Mr. Jones do their jobs, then they are men," Cade said.

"Damn right," Rollins said.

"Now, to get on with it. You'll all be staying in the bunkhouse, and the Colonel will be feeding you while you're here. I know a few of you are short of money, but you won't be needing to spend anything while you're here."

"What about beer 'n pretty girls? Is the Colonel gonna provide that?" Muley Morris asked.

Cade and the other cowboys chuckled. "My guess would be, no."

"Well then, I'm goin' to have to spend a little money, 'cause I don't aim on settin' out on any three-month trip without somethin' to remember while I'm gone."

"I'm afraid, gentlemen, that you will be on your own, on that score."

The gather for the drive was made somewhat easier because the other ranchers, who were bringing their cattle to join the herd, had already done the roundups at their own ranches, separating the cows that would go, from those that would stay.

Each cowboy going north was assigned at least five horses, and counting Cade and Jeter, that meant that no less than seventy horses would be making the drive. One man would be assigned the job of horse wrangler, and Cade selected Timmy Ponder.

If the cow ponies were well trained, they would stand in position for a long time, the reins having been dropped to the ground in front of their feet. The goal was that the horse and rider would be comfortable with each other, so the first week at the ranch was generally spent with the cowboys selecting and getting to know the string of ponies they would be riding. Then the wrangler would work to acclimate the animals to a rope corral that would enclose the horses at night.

The next order of business was to apply a road brand to every cow in the herd. This unifying brand made the recognition and counting of the cows much easier, and the physical application was much simpler. The cattle were driven through a chute, and a large two-headed arrow, which was the brand chosen by the owners of the combined herd, was applied on the side of the cow.

"Have you found him yet?" Cade asked as he brought his horse to a stop beside Jeter. The branding operation was in process and the protesting bawl of the animals was in the background, making it hard to hear one another.

"Not yet," Jeter said. "I'll give 'em all another look through; maybe one of 'em will jump out at me."

"What ya'll lookin' for?" GW Jones asked.

Jeter raised his eyebrows and turned to Cade for his response. Most trail bosses might consider GW's question impertinent but Cade knew the boy couldn't learn if he didn't observe, and ask questions.

"We're looking for the most dominating steer in the entire herd," Cade said.

"What for?"

"Once we find him, we'll put him in front; then the others will follow him."

"Oh, well, if that's what you're lookin' for, that would be him, right there." Jones pointed to a big, reddish-brown steer. He had an enormous spread of horns, at least seven feet from tip to tip. "He's been bossin' the others around ever since he got here. I call him Goliath."

"Goliath, huh?"

"Yes, sir."

"You think he can get the other cows to follow him?"

"I know he can."

"All right, I'm going to leave that up to you. Cut 'im out, we'll get him ready."

"You want me to cut him out of the herd?"

"Think you can do that?"

GW smiled broadly. "Mr. McCall, you just watch. I got me the best cuttin' horse in the whole bunch."

GW saddled, then mounted his horse, and rode into the herd. Heading toward Goliath, horse and rider began to move as if sharing the same musculature, twisting, turning, making sudden stops, then darting forward, varying the pace.

"That boy is one hell of rider," Cade said.

"I told you he was," Jeter said. "Remember, he's the boy who snatched a handkerchief up from the road, while he was ridin' full gallop." Jeter turned his horse and rode toward GW.

Once Goliath was clear of the herd, Jeter had his lariat whirling over his head. He let the rope play out until he had an oval shaped noose, some seven feet in diameter. Just before he made the throw, he drew his arm and shoulder back, then shot his hand forward. The noose cleared Goliath's horns, and fell down around Goliath's neck. The giant steer fought against it, but Jeter wrapped his end of the rope around the saddle horn. He was riding a horse that was well trained and experienced for these situations, and it squatted down on its back legs so that when the steer hauled back on the rope, it was held tight.

By now Cade had joined them, and he, too, dropped a rope around the steer's neck. When Goliath realized he couldn't fight both of them, he quit trying and allowed them to put him into a separate pen. When he settled down, Jeter turned in ten relatively domesticated cows and watched as Goliath began to dominate the others. The purpose of this was to allow Goliath to establish his leadership, and when they started the drive, with ten of the cows already following Goliath, the rest of the herd would tend to fall in behind.

"Oh, no, is that Weldon?" Art Finley asked when the chuck wagon came into sight. "If I'd knowed he was gonna be our cookie, I might not have signed up."

"I tried," Cade said. "Believe me, I tried."

"All right, I guess we survived his cookin' last year, so we can do it again, but I can tell you one damned thing, I ain't gonna be happy."

"I know," Cade said, "but he's the one. Now that he's here, get your gear ready, and if any of you have a mind to go into town, now's the time to do it. I'm thinking we'll be getting underway first thing tomorrow morning."

"Yahoo!" a couple of the cowboys yelled.

"Last year we would've been right with 'em," Jeter said as he watched the men scatter.

"But not this year," Cade said. "I expect you'll want to tell Maggie goodbye, won't you?"

"You're damn right I do!"

"Well then, what do you say we head over to the MW for this one, last night?"

"Do you think they'll have somethin' special cooked for us?" Jeter asked.

"I don't know," Cade replied as a smile crossed his face. "You think the sun will come up in the East tomorrow morning?"

Eight of the cowboys went into town on their last night. It was nine, if you counted Weldon, but he was a cook, not a cowboy, and neither he, nor the cowboys thought of him in any other way.

"Yes, sir," GW was telling the others. "We won't have to do nothin' but just ride alongside 'em, 'n them cows will walk up to Abilene near 'bout all by themselves."

"Now, just how the hell is that goin' to happen?" Timmy Ponder asked.

"Goliath is goin' to lead 'em all the way. 'N I'm the one that handpicked 'im, and I'm the one that cut 'im out of the herd too."

"GW, you're as full of shit as a Christmas goose," Troy Hastings said.

"No, he's right," Boo Rollins said. "On ever' drive, the first thing you do is choose the steer that the other cows will follow."

"Well, I'll be damn," Troy said. "Who would 'a ever thought of somethin' like that?"

The eight cowboys—Boo Rollins, Art Finley, Petey Malone, Muley Morris, Mo Bender, Timmy Ponder, Troy Hastings, and GW Jones, were holding their conversation in the Bit and Spur Saloon. Ike Weldon had come into the bar as well but he was sitting at a table apart from the others.

The Bit and Spur was a lively place. The piano player, an unlit cigar protruding from his mouth, was wearing a bowler hat and a white shirt, with garters around his sleeves. He shifted the cigar from side to side as he pounded away on the piano. Whether the off-key notes were the result of the piano being out of tune, or the lack of skill by the pianist, no one could discern. Some were aware of the frequent inharmonious notes however, and the clients who actually had an appreciation of music would cringe until the discordant interlude had passed.

"I'm goin' to get me a beer," Ponder said. "I ain't never had me no beer before, but now that I'm a man, I aim to get me one."

"Ha! You're a long way from bein' a man," Petey Malone said.

"Leave 'im alone, Malone. As long as anyone rides with us, he's a man," Boo Rollins said, resolutely.

"Where's Weldon?" Mo Bender asked.

"Do you expect a cook to be with common cowboys?" Morris asked. "Look at 'im over there in the corner, talkin' to the ladies."

"Looks like all the ladies are really a' likin' 'im," Jones said.

"Boy, as you get a little older, you'll learn that the ladies like any man who has money in his pocket."

"Where'd Weldon get money? We ain't been paid yet," Hastings said.

"He gets enough money to put the chuck wagon together a' fore we leave," Rollins explained. "If he shops real smart, he'll sometimes have a little left over."

"You mean if he don't spend enough money to feed us proper," Finley said. "They's a reason they call 'em belly robbers."

Timmy Ponder returned to the others, carrying a glass of whiskey.

"Damn, Timmy, when you said you was goin' to get a drink, I figured it would be a beer."

"No, I've actual had me a beer before," Ponder replied. "But I figured I'd have me a man's drink tonight."

He turned the glass up to his lips and took a deep swallow. Immediately thereafter he spewed it out in a coughing, hacking spray.

The others laughed.

"How do you like it?" GW asked.

With a sheepish grin, Ponder put the glass down on the table. "I think I'll get me a beer," he said.

MW Ranch:

Maggie wanted to cook something special for them on their last night, so she cooked beef that she had marinated in red wine. Beef Bourguignon.

"Oh, Lord a' mighty, this is the best thing I've ever tasted in my life," Jeter said. "And you're tellin' me this came from a cow?"

"*Oui,*" Maggie said. "Yes," she added with a little laugh.

"I've been around cows all my life, I had no idea you could get meat like this from a cow."

"It isn't the meat, it's the way the meat is prepared," Arabella said. "It's called Beef Bourguignon."

"I don't care what you're gonna call it, it sure is good," Jeter said as he tore off a piece of hot sourdough bread and dunked it in the juices.

"I'm glad you like it, Monsieur Jeter," Maggie said.

"Can't we drop the *mon sewer* thing, and you just call me Jeter?"

Maggie smiled. "*Oui* . . . Zheter."

They had finished their meal and Maggie was getting their desert, when there was a loud knock on the door.

"Mr. McCall! Mr. Willis!"

"That's Boo Rollins, isn't it?" Cade asked.

"Sounds like 'im. I wonder what he wants?" Jeter said.

"There's only one way to find out," Cade said as he headed for the door.

Rollins was standing there, with a very troubled look on his face.

"Boo, what is it? What's wrong?"

"We got trouble, Mr. McCall. We got bad trouble. I 'spect you'd better come back to Texana with me."

"What's happened?"

"It's Weldon. He's in Texana. Actually, he's in jail in Texana is where he is."

Sheriff Boskey shook his head. "There's nothin' I can do about it, Cade. Weldon 'n a man by the name of Meacham got into a row about some whores over in the Bit and Spur, 'n the next thing anyone knew, Weldon grabbed a chair 'n brung it down hard on Meacham's head. I'm holdin' Weldon for assault and battery, but if Meacham dies, it could be murder."

"Is Meacham likely to die?" Cade asked.

"I don't know. Right now he's down at Doc Presnell's office. The doc said he got his skull broke, 'n that's real serious. You can see how I can't let Weldon go, can't you?"

"Yeah," Cade replied quietly. "Yeah, I can see why you can't let him go. Damn."

"Does this put you in a tight position?" Boskey asked.

"I'd say it does. We'd planned to head out tomorrow, but now I'll have to find a cook."

"I'm sorry," Boskey said.

"No need for you to be sorry, Sheriff. You were just doing your job. It's Weldon who is sorry, and I don't mean apologetic. He's just one sorry-assed son of a bitch."

Victoria:

Amon Kilgore was having a beer with a whore named Blissful in the Last Chance Saloon, when he saw someone come in that he didn't expect to see.

"What are you doing here?" Kilgore asked. "I thought you were leaving tomorrow."

"We gotta talk," Jeremiah Mudd said.

"Honey, maybe you didn't notice, but I'm already talkin' to 'im," Blissful said.

"This is important," Mudd said.

Kilgore drummed his fingers on the table for a moment, then took out a five-dollar bill and gave it to Blissful. "Will this hold you for few minutes while me 'n my friend talk in private?" he asked.

A broad smile spread across Blissful's face. "Honey you just bought yourself as much privacy as you want," she said.

Kilgore watched her walk away with an exaggerated swing of her rear end.

"You ever seen an ass like that?" Kilgore asked.

"Weldon's in jail," Mudd said, not responding to Kilgore, but getting right to the point.

"What?"

"He tried to kill someone."

"That dumb son of a bitch! What's gonna happen now?"

"The drive sure as hell ain't goin' to start 'til McCall 'n Willis find 'em a new cook."

"Damn! Do you have any idea who they might get?"

"Hell no. If they can't find somebody they'll likely pawn it off on that old fart, Campbell."

"That'll make it harder."

"It don't matter who the new cook is. It don't even matter that Weldon's in jail. What was he gonna do anyway? He didn't make the deal for us to get twenty dollars a head, now did he? And he wasn't goin' to be no help cuttin' out the five hundred cows Gorman said he could take, now was he?"

Kilgore nodded. "You're right. We don't need him. But, what if the son of a bitch starts talkin'? What if he decides he can bargain his way out of jail if he tells what we got planned?"

"He won't talk."

"How do you know he won't talk?"

"I promise you, he won't talk," Mudd said again.

12

Indianola was the county seat of Calhoun County, with a population of nearly five thousand people. It was a bustling community which competed with Galveston as a port city, and when Cade rode into town, the street was full of wagons, buckboards, and carriages. He dismounted in front of the sheriff's office.

"Yes, sir, what can I do for you?" the sheriff asked.

"Sheriff, my name is Cade McCall, from over in Jackson County. I'm putting together a cattle drive through to Kansas, and because of circumstances, the cook I had planned on using is no longer available. I got a lead on someone here who might be a possibility. His name is Willie Tyrone. Do you know anything about him?"

The sheriff chuckled. "I know two things about him. He's a very good cook, and right now he's half way to England."

"What?"

"He signed on to sail with the *Texas Star*."

"What about Moses Joiner?"

"You willin' to pay his bail?"

"He's in jail?"

"He tends to spend a lot of time in my jail," the sheriff said.

Cade shook his head. "No thanks, that's the problem with the one I have now."

"You might try Ron Trapp. Right now he's ridin' shotgun for the Coastal Stage, but he's done some cookin' in the past. I think he made a drive a couple of years ago for Richard King."

"Is he out on a trip right now, or is he in town?"

"He's in town; doesn't leave until tomorrow. I saw him down at the depot about an hour ago."

Trapp was drinking coffee with some of the team handlers when Cade went into the stage depot.

"Mr. Trapp, my name is Cade McCall, I'm a cattle drive contractor, and I'm looking for a cook."

"You're wantin' to hire me, are you?"

"Well, I certainly want to talk to you about it," Cade said.

"When are you leavin'?"

Cade smiled. "Well, that all depends on when I get a cook. But as soon as possible."

"If you'd put it off for a month, I'll cook for you."

"Put it off for a month?"

"Yeah." Trapp smiled. "I got me a mail-order bride comin' in, in a couple of weeks, 'n I wouldn't want to get married then run off 'n leave her, first thing. Besides which if you leave too soon, why, I might not be here when she gets here, 'n what if she ups 'n marries somebody else? I figure if you would wait a month though, it would all work out."

Cade shook his head. "Sorry, Mr. Trapp, you've made trail drives; you know how it is. The quicker we get there, the better the price. I'm afraid I can't wait a month."

"Then I can't cook for you," Trapp said. "Truth is, I'm not all that sure I want to, anyway. Ridin' shotgun on a stage coach don't pay as much, but it ain't as tirin' 'n you ain't never gone more 'n a few days at a time; nothin' like a three or four month trail drive." Trapp turned away and lifted the coffee cup to his mouth, by way of dismissal.

From Indianola, Cade rode to Wharton, where he heard there were two possibilities. One of the prospects was working as a clerk in a clothing store, and he didn't want to leave the comfort and safety of such a job. When the other prospect was pointed out to Cade he saw a man who was so filthy that Cade felt dirty, just by looking at him. He rode away without even approaching him.

As Cade was riding back to Texana, frustrated because he'd been unable to find a cook, he saw a man sitting on a horse in the road ahead of him. Even from here he could see that it was a very big man and he realized, rather quickly, that this was Bull Kolinsky, the man he had bested a few days earlier.

Cade knew he had won that fight because he had the element of surprise. He doubted, seriously, if he would be able to surprise this man again. Reaching down to his side, he loosened the pistol in its holster. He didn't want to kill Bull, but if the big man wanted revenge for what had happened to him in their last meeting, shooting him might be Cade's only safe option. The truth was, in a direct head to head confrontation, he wouldn't stand a chance against the giant.

"McCall?" Bull called, the low rumble of his voice rolling across the distance between them.

Cade stopped before he got any closer.

"What do you want, Bull?"

"The fight me 'n you had?"

"Yes?"

"Kilgore paid me to fight you, on account of he wanted you hurt so's you couldn't make the drive."

"What difference would it make to him whether or not I make the drive?"

"I don't know, he didn't say. All he said was that he didn't want you to make the drive."

"Bull, why are you telling me this?"

"I don't know. I guess because you beat me fair and square. And besides which, the son of a bitch cheated me. Anyhow, I just thought I'd tell you."

Without another word, Bull turned and rode off.

"What do you suppose he meant by that?" Jeter asked, after Cade shared his conversation with Bull.

"I don't know. All he said was Kilgore didn't want me to make the drive."

"Yeah, well, as far as I'm concerned, I'd be keeping my eyes on Kilgore anyway. I never did like the son of a bitch."

"Let's not say anything about this in front of the women," Cade said. "Arabella's already nervous about us being gone. I don't see any need in giving them something else to worry about."

The two men were treated to another exceptional dinner that evening, one that had both of them requesting seconds.

About half way through the meal, Arabella spoke up. "Magnolia and I were wondering if you found your new cook."

Cade took a deep breath and let out a sigh. "No luck at all. Several people gave me good suggestions, but nobody agreed to sign on. I even went back and tried to talk Waters into coming with us, but he still says he thinks he's not up to it. And Rand, even when I offered to match the salary he's getting at the hotel, still turned me down. And to be honest, I guess I can't blame him. He said if he leaves his job, he wouldn't get it back again when he got back."

"You know he's right. I can't see Oliver Deermont being generous enough to just hire him back on," Jeter said. "So, where does that leave us? What do we do now?"

"I have no idea. We have to feed the men, but at the moment, I'm at my wit's end," Cade said. "I'll give it one more day, and then I'll have to draft Ian. He'd probably do a better job than any of the other drovers."

Arabella and Maggie exchanged looks.

"Shall I?" Arabella asked.

Maggie nodded.

"Shall you what?" Cade asked. "What's going on here?"

"Magnolia and I have an idea," Arabella said.

"You aren't going to ask us to call off the drive, are you? Because we can't do that. After the losses from the hurricane, the cattlemen are depending on this drive to keep many of them from losing their ranches. And quite frankly, Jeter and I need the money as well."

"No, that's not what we have in mind."

"Then, what is it?"

"You need a cook? Well open your eyes, Cade McCall. You don't have to look any further."

"What do you mean?"

"*Mon Dieu,* Cade, are you really that dense? Magnolia and I will be your cooks."

"What?" Cade asked, barking the word in surprise.

"You said yourself that you're in desperate need of a cook. Can you not see that the answer is right here in front of you? Take us with you."

"No, we couldn't do that," Cade replied. "That's out of the question."

"Why not?" Arabella asked. "You've been sitting here for the last half hour, talking about getting a cook . . . this after eating a meal that Magnolia and I prepared for you. I no longer have a boarding house to operate, and that means that Magnolia and I are both out of work. We need a job, and you need a cook." Arabella smiled, broadly. "Don't you see how wonderfully that all works out? Magnolia and I will cook for you."

"Women on a cattle drive? No," Cade said. "You understand you'd be living in a wagon for two or three months, and you'd be cooking over an open fire for at least twelve or fifteen people every day. And there wouldn't be any store to go to when you run out of something."

"Oh, for heaven's sake, Cade, thousands of women went West on wagon trains, didn't they?"

"Yes."

"Then how is this any different?"

"There were other women on the wagon trains."

"There'll be other women on this drive," Arabella insisted.

"What do you mean, there'll be other women?"

"Magnolia will be the other woman for me, and I'll be the other woman for her."

Cade laughed. "Well, I can't argue with that, now can I?"

Jeter shook his head as he spoke for the first time. "A woman cook on a cattle drive? I've never heard of such a thing."

"Would you like some more Crème Caramel, Zheter?" Maggie asked as she pushed forward the rich desert she had made for dinner.

"Oh, yes, I'd love some more. That's about the best tasting thing I've ever put in my mou . . ." Jeter stopped in mid-sentence and smiled at Maggie. "Wait a minute," he said. "I see what you're doing."

Cade stroked his chin and looked over at Jeter. "What do you say, Jeter?"

"They're right when they say we're going to need a cook, and I've never known a trail cook who could cook like this. If we're votin' on it . . . I would say yes."

"All right," Cade said. "I may wind up regretting this, and you two may wind up regretting it even more. But if you're serious, if you really want to cook for the cattle drive, I say you're hired. Oh, and by the way, if you two are going to be doing a man's work, you're going to have to dress for it, so you may as well go into town tomorrow and buy yourselves some men's clothes to wear."

"All right," Arabella agreed, a big smile crossing her face.

"You mean you aren't going to argue about that?"

"*Tu es le patron,*" Arabella said, sweetly.

"What?"

"You're the boss," she translated.

"Yes, I am, aren't I?" Cade said with a wide smile. "And you remember that, too."

"I'm sorry we'll be delaying your start while we go into town to buy clothes," Arabella said.

"That's not the only thing that's stopping us," Cade said.

"Oh? What else do we need to get?"

Cade smiled. "Arabella, if you're going to be making this drive with us, you'll be doing it as my wife. We're getting married before we leave."

Texana:

The buildings blocked any of the light from the street lamps coming through, and there was no ambient light from the back of the buildings. As a result, the alley was very dark. There were several outhouses placed along the alley, and as Mudd walked down it, the door to one of the outhouses opened, and he saw a man, hooking his galluses over his shoulders, one shoulder at a time. Mudd waited, secure that in the darkness he couldn't be seen, then he continued on down the alley until he reached the back of the jail.

"Weldon," he called in a loud whisper. "Weldon!"

"What?" a disembodied voice came from inside the jail.

"Weldon, come to the back window."

"You're gettin' me out?"

"Yeah. Come back here."

Weldon's face appeared in the window. Even in the darkness, he could be seen smiling.

"Mudd! How are you goin' to get me out of here?"

"This way," Mudd said, reaching one hand through the window to grab Weldon's hair and pull him closer to the bars.

"What are you . . .?" That was as far as he got because the knife in Mudd's other hand slit his throat.

The next morning Deputy O'Connor stepped back into the cell area, carrying a plate. "All right, Weldon, I got your breakfast here, 'n from what I've heard about your cookin', this is likely to be better 'n anythin' you could do."

O'Connor laughed at his own joke, and then he saw Weldon lying on the floor under the back window. At first he was puzzled seeing him there, instead of on the bed, and he was even more puzzled by his position. Nobody would lie with his arms and legs askew in such a fashion.

"Weldon, what are you doing there on the floor?"

Weldon didn't answer.

"Son of a bitch!" O'Connor said. He stepped back out front to get the keys for the cell, but then had a second thought. What if Weldon was just lying like that to trick him? He decided he had better get Sheriff Boskey, just in case.

Sheriff Boskey was having his breakfast at the café next door when O'Connor told him what he had found. Boskey left his breakfast uneaten to hurry back to the jail with his deputy.

"I didn't want to go in there by myself," Deputy O'Connor said. "You know, just in case it was a trick, or somethin'."

"You did the right thing by coming for me," Sheriff Boskey said.

Boskey got the keys and unlocked the cell door. O'Connor waited just outside the cell while Boskey made a quick observation.

"It's no trick," Boskey said. "Someone cut his throat. He's dead."

"But how? I mean, he didn't have no visitors for the whole night," O'Connor said. "How did somebody get in here to cut his throat?"

Boskey looked up at the window and saw blood on the sill of the window, and on the bars.

"He had a visitor all right," Boskey said. "Only thing is, his didn't come inside."

13

The LP Ranch:

When Agnes Puckett learned that Cade and Arabella planned to go to the justice of the peace in Texana to be married, she said, in no way, would they be married that way. She insisted on having the wedding at the LP Ranch, and she sent someone into town after the Reverend E.D. Owen. As she waited on the preacher, she began making arrangements to hold the wedding in the parlor.

"What are you going to wear?" Agnes asked Arabella.

"I . . . haven't actually given that any thought," Arabella said. "We were just going to get married in town, so I thought I would get married in what I'm wearing."

"Good heavens, girl, you're wearing trousers! Is that what you're planning to wear for your wedding?"

"Yes, ma'am, Cade said trousers would be more appropriate for the drive."

"For the drive, perhaps. But we aren't talking about the drive; we're talking about the wedding." A broad smile spread across her face. "And I have just the thing for you. I still have the wedding gown I was married in."

By the time Reverend Owen arrived, the parlor had been transformed, if not into a church, at least into a wedding chapel. Here and there were bouquets of Texas wildflowers. The cowboys who would be making the drive were, to the man, present. All the cowboys showed up wearing their cleanest trousers, as well as their white shirts that were usually reserved for their night out on the town. Only the two Mexican "vaqueros", Esteban Garcia and Alberto Tangora were dressed differently, each of them wearing black trousers, a black shirt, and a colorful sash tied around the waist.

Most were standing around self-consciously, drinking black coffee. Reverend Owen, after being introduced to the two he would be marrying, accepted a cup of coffee and sat drinking as Agnes got the cowboys situated where they could all see.

"Preacher, are you ready to marry these two?" Colonel Puckett asked.

"As soon as I finish my coffee," the preacher replied with a beatific smile.

There was no music, and no procession of the bride. Arabella was wearing Mrs. Puckett's ivory-colored dress with a high neck and rows of lace and Cade was dressed in his best white shirt, the only difference from any of the other men was the attachment of a collar. They stood in the wide doorway that led from the parlor into the dining room. Maggie, as bridesmaid, and Jeter as best man, stood with them.

Reverend Owen stepped in front of them, and then began the ceremony.

"Dearly beloved, we are gathered here in the sight of God and these witnesses to join this man and this woman in holy matrimony."

The preacher's remarks continued until he gave the statement of intention, and now at Reverend Owen's instruction, Cade turned to Arabella, taking her hands in his.

"I, Cade McCall, take you, Arabella Dupree, to be my wife, to have and to hold, from this day forward, for better or for worse, for richer or for poorer, in sickness and in health, to love and to cherish, excluding all others, as long as we both shall live."

Cade gave Arabella's hands a little squeeze, and she replied.

"I, Arabella Dupree, take you, Cade McCall, to be my husband, to love, honor and obey, from this day forward, for better or for worse, for richer or for poorer, in sickness and in health, to love and to cherish, excluding all others, as long as we both shall live."

"The ring," Reverend Owen said, looking directly at Jeter. When Jeter didn't respond, Reverend Owen spoke again. "Mr. Willis?"

"What?"

"The ring?"

"Oh, uh, yeah, the ring." Jeter reached into his pocket, pulled out the ring and gave it to Cade, who slipped it onto Arabella's finger.

The minister concluded the ceremony. "And now, by the authority invested in me as a minister of the Gospel, and in accordance with the laws of the State of Texas, I pronounce you man and wife. You may kiss the bride."

Jeter was the first to give a toast.

"Arabella, hold your hand out, palm up," Jeter said.

Arabella responded.

"Cade put your hand over hers."

Cade took Arabella's hand in his.

"Now, Cade, I want you to remember this solemn moment, because this is the last time you will ever have the upper hand."

The others laughed.

"*Qu'il y ait toujours l'amour entre vous.*" Maggie said, then she translated. "Let there always be love between you."

There were other toasts as well, including one by Alberto Tangora. "*Que tu amor sólo crecer a partir de este día en Adelante.*" And as Maggie had before him, he translated. "May your love only grow from this day forth."

"Sure now 'n here's a Scottish blessing for ye," Ian Campbell said. "May the best day the two of ye have ever seen be the worst you'll ever see."

With the toasts and blessings completed, the cowboys gathered around the table where, on short order, and with Maggie's help, pastries had been prepared.

"I thought maybe Jeter was going to keep the ring for himself," Boo Rollins teased.

"No, I wasn't goin' to do anything like that," Jeter said. "I guess I was just so taken with what was happening, I mean, Cade gettin' married 'n all, that I wasn't thinking."

"Tell me, Mrs. McCall..." Reverend Owen started to say.

"Oh! That's the first time I've ever been addressed as Mrs. McCall," Arabella said, with a broad, beaming smile. She reached over to take Cade's hand. "It has such a wonderful sound to it."

"You'll get used to it, my dear," Agnes Puckett said. "And it will get very comfortable."

"Oh, I'm already comfortable with it." She looked back at the preacher. "Pardon me, Reverend, you were about to ask a question and I interrupted you. I'm so sorry. What is the question?"

"I was just going to ask if it is true that you'll be going on the cattle drive."

"*Oui.* And I'm very much looking forward to it. I think it will be a wonderful adventure."

Jeter and Maggie stayed at the LP, while Cade and Arabella rode back to the MW to spend their first night as husband and wife. It wasn't the first time Cade and Arabella had been together, but it was the first time in a long time, and they very much appreciated the opportunity, and the privacy.

Afterward, they lay next to each other, coasting down from their recent bliss, enjoying the closeness.

"Have you ever looked back over your life, at the twists and turns it makes until it gets you to the point where you are now?" Cade asked. "I was a farmer, a soldier, a prisoner of war, a sailor . . . and now I am here, starting my married life with you."

Arabella chuckled. "I don't have to look any further back than the day I got twenty dollars from Monsieur Lundy when I arranged for you to be shanghaied. Little did I know that, one day you and I would be married. I will never forgive myself for that."

"I'm glad it happened," Cade said. "If it hadn't happened, we wouldn't be lying here, together, now would we?"

"Oh, quelle toile nous tissons."

"What?"

"What a web we weave," Maggie translated.

Cade laughed. "I'm like Jeter, I'm going to have to learn French."

The drovers who would make the drive had been bunking at the LP while Cade and Jeter were making preparations to leave. It had not created a problem because the bunkhouse was nearly empty, as so many hands had moved on after the hurricane.

Agnes Puckett and her hired girl, Fernanda Lopez, had been cooking for the ranch for many years, so it was an easy thing for them to cook for the extra men, and now they were helped by Maggie Trudeau. Maggie, of course, was an excellent cook, but she appreciated learning how to cook for a group of hungry drovers.

"You're a wonderful cook, dear," Agnes Puckett said, "but on the trail, you won't have access to all the ingredients you can get when you're close to a town. Your most valuable piece of equipment is your Dutch oven."

"My Dutch oven?"

"Yes. You'll bake your biscuits in it, and you'll make your stews and beans in the same pot. When you're crossing a river, you make sure you know where this pot is at all times, because if you lose it, you'll have a hard time fixing any meal."

"I'll take care of it," Maggie said.

"And you do know that you'll be doing all your cooking over an open fire. Make sure to use your coals. If you're cooking beans, bury your Dutch oven the night before and make sure that when the night hawks come in, you have them put coals on top of the lid. Then in the morning, your beans are cooked."

"Oh Mrs. Puckett, do you think Arabella and I can do this? There is so much to learn."

"Don't worry my dear," Mrs. Puckett said as she patted Maggie's shoulder. "The boys want you to succeed. They'll help you any way they can. Oh, there's one more thing you need to know. Anytime you see any wood along the way, stop and gather what you can. Keep it in the coonie—that's a cow skin that's attached under the wagon, and if you don't find enough wood, have your horse wrangler help you pick up cow chips along the way."

"Cow chips? I don't know cow chips."

"Well, they are . . . uh . . .they are, things that you will be in no short supply of. They actually make a better fire than wood."

"And I will find this marvelous fuel on the prairie?"

"You will find it anywhere cattle have been. When the cattle move on, they leave the chips behind them."

"Oh!" Maggie said, putting her hand to her mouth. "Are you talking about *merde?*"

"Honey, I'm not sure of your French," Agnes said. "But, yes, I'm pretty sure we are talking about the same thing."

"And you say you can use these . . .turds . . .to cook with?"

Agnes laughed. "Now I know we are talking about the same thing. And yes, they are very good for making a fire you can cook with. They burn clean, with absolutely no odor."

14

Victoria, Texas:

We'll be headin' out tomorrow morning," Jeremiah Mudd said.

"Good," Amon Kilgore said. "Did you have any trouble slipping away tonight?"

"Not at all. Ever body's actin' like it's Christmas out at the LP," Mudd said. "McCall got married last night, 'n he wants to spend more time with his bride, so he 'n Willis gave everyone one last night to come to town."

"All right. You be one of the first ones to get back out there, so nobody notices you didn't go to the Bit and Spur with 'em."

"How many men are in on this?" Mudd asked.

"They'll be five countin' you," Kilgore said. "We'll be scoutin' the best place to hit."

"I can tell you where that'll be. The Lavaca River. The herd will be all strung out when we're fordin', 'n by the time three quarters are across, that'll leave just about the number of cows you said you wanted," Mudd said. "And, here's somethin' else. We've got two or three drovers that ain't dry behind the ears yet. More 'n likely they'll be the ones left to get those last cows across."

"And where will you be?" Kilgore asked.

"I'll see if I can't trade places with one of the young 'ns. They won't want to be eatin' that dust if they can get on over in the front."

Kilgore smiled. "You're a good man, Jeremiah."

LP Ranch:

By the time dawn broke on the morning the drive was to start, the air was rich with the aroma of coffee and fried ham. Maggie had brioche French toast, and served it with butter and molasses.

"This is quite an undertaking for a trail drive breakfast, isn't it?" Cade asked, though he helped himself to a generous portion.

"Magnolia and I thought it would be something nice to serve to the men on the first day," Arabella replied.

"Now, Cade, don't you go interfering," Jeter said as he put three pieces of the French toast onto his own plate. "I think this is a fine breakfast,"

Cade chuckled. "Apparently, everyone else does as well."

After breakfast, as they were preparing to leave, everyone on the ranch turned out to see them off. The cattle, gathered with other cows that were unfamiliar, sensed that their life had changed in some significant way, and they milled about nervously. The milling around lifted a large cloud of dust, which caught the morning sun and gleamed in a bright gold.

Every cowboy who would be making the drive was mounted, and helping to get 2,250 cows herded together for the long push north.

Goliath, the large steer that GW Jones had selected, was brought to the front of the herd.

"All right, boys, let's get 'em movin'!" Cade shouted.

Finally the cattle were gathered, and under the urging of the cowboys, began the slow, shuffling walk that were the first steps of the more than seven hundred miles that lay between them and Abilene, Kansas. Soon, the cattle fell into place, moving like soldiers on parade with each cow keeping the same relative position within the file.

At the beginning, the herd wasn't pushed very hard, but was allowed to graze and to grow comfortable in their new environment. Cade rode along with the herd for the first couple of hours, then leaving Jeter in charge, and with all the cowboys in their proper place, he slapped his legs against the side of his horse and urged it into a gallop, dashing alongside the slowly moving cows until he topped a small hill where he stopped to look back down on the herd. They made an impressive sight, the line stretching out. From this position Cade could see the entire herd, with a steer's head and horns silhouetted against the skyline, and then another, and another still, stretching on back along the trail for three quarters of a mile.

Timmy Ponder was riding about 1000 yards in front of the cattle, herding the just over 70 horses, which throughout the drive would be rotated with the horses the cowboys were riding.

Rollins was at the head of the herd, Ian Campbell was the flank rider on the left side, near the front, and Muley Morris was the first swing rider on the same side, somewhat farther back. Art Finley was riding flank on the right side, with Petey Malone in the first swing position. The rest of the cowboys, Esteban Garcia, Alberto Tangora, Mo Bender and Jerimiah Mudd were positioned on either side of the herd. To Troy Hastings and GW Jones, went the thankless job of riding drag. Cade could barely see them in the dust that was being kicked up by the herd.

Jeter had no fixed position, but was moving all around the herd, keeping his eye on the operation.

Arabella and Maggie were driving the chuck wagon, which was already a couple of miles ahead of the herd. They would continue on until they found a good place to stop for the camp. They had studied a map with Cade, who had made this drive before, and planned to stop at Boggy Creek, where there would be water and grass. Once the cattle were stopped it would take no effort to hold them there because if there was grass and water, they would be perfectly content to stay where they were until they were forced to move on.

Coming down from the hill, Cade put the horse into an easy loping run until he saw the chuck wagon in front of him. Behind the wagon was the two-wheeled hoodlum wagon that would be carrying all the bedrolls, extra saddles, and tools—ax, shovel, branding iron—or anything else that may be needed.

As he came closer he heard Arabella and Maggie's voices, and for a moment he was puzzled, until he realized they were singing.

> *Alouette, gentille alouette,*
> *Alouette, je te plumerai.*
> *Je te plumerai la tête*
> *Je te plumerai la tête*
> *Et la tête Et la tête*
> *Alouette, Alouette*

Cade had heard them singing the song before, so he picked up on it, singing loudly as he rode up to join them.

> *Ahhhhhh Alouette, gentille alouette,*
> *Alouette, je te plumerai.*

Both women were laughing when Cade rode up beside them, and they finished the song together.

"Maybe I've got you two ladies in the wrong place," Cade said. "I should have you riding alongside the cows. They like beautiful music you know; it keeps them quiet."

"Oh, but it won't work, Cade," Arabella insisted. "It would never do for Maggie and me to sing to the cows."

"Why not?"

"Because, silly, they don't understand French."

Cade laughed out loud. "I guess you may have a point there."

"Oh, there's the creek ahead," Maggie said.

"The herd will be here in about another three hours," Cade said. "Will that give you time to fix lunch?"

"*Oui*," Maggie said. "We will have fried steak au jus, with mashed potatoes and biscuits."

"Don't bring this up to me at some later time, but I'm glad I couldn't find another cook." He turned, to rejoin the herd.

"Cade?" Arabella called to him.

"Yes."

"Are you going to leave without giving me a kiss?"

Cade smiled. "I'm not about to." Leaning down from the saddle, he kissed Arabella who was sitting on the wagon seat.

"Lord, Mr. McCall, we goin' to eat like this ever' day?" Boo Rollins asked. "Even with Mr. Slade, we most just had cold biscuits 'n bacon for the noon meals."

"We'll probably have our share of cold biscuits on this drive as well," Cade said. "But I think our cooks are just trying to get used to their jobs."

"I'll say one thing, I hope they don't get used to it too quick," Art Finley said, and the others laughed.

Supper that evening was just as memorable; it was beef and potato stew. For the entire day, Maggie had been carrying beans in a pot of water, and now she added chunks of pork, onions, and peppers to the Dutch oven, then buried it near the fire, putting the hot coals over the top, just as Mrs. Puckett had explained.

Petey Malone got his guitar from the Hoodlum wagon, and he, Art Finley, Muley Morris, and Boo Rollins began singing *I'll Take You Home Again*, their voices blending perfectly.

Cade had spread out a blanket and he and Arabella were sitting on it, leaning back against the wheel of the chuck wagon, listening to the music. Tiny, glowing red embers were riding heat waves from the fire, high enough into the velvet black sky that it looked as if they were joining with the sparkling stars that winked down from above. Cade had his arm around her shoulders.

"Oh," Arabella said. "I thought you said that the drive would be very difficult. This is . . . *merveilleux, magnifique*! Is it always so?"

"No, not always," Cade said. He pulled her closer to him. "I've never had you with me, before."

"Tangora 'n Bender, you two have the first night-hawk duty," Jeter said. "You'd better get out there."

Though most of the men had thrown their bedrolls out on the ground around the fire, Cade had made a special place for him and Arabella by stretching canvas out on the ground under the wagon, then draping canvas down around the sides to provide some privacy for Arabella. Maggie was inside the wagon. She had her bedroll rolled out over the sacks of flour and beans, and it was private as well as quite comfortable.

The next several days passed without incident, then on noon of the eighth day, as Arabella and Maggie prepared to move ahead to the night encampment, Cade told Jeter that he would be going with them.

"I'm a little worried about the Lavaca River. Sometimes it can be hard for a wagon to ford, and Arabella hasn't had that much experience handling the mules. I'll ride along beside to see to it that all goes well," Cade said. "Then when I get them across, I'll come back to help the herd cross."

"Good idea," Jeter replied, looking up to the sky to see the position of the sun. "If we can get there by four, we should have plenty of daylight to water the entire herd and get them across."

Amon Kilgore, Fred Toombs, Elvis Graves and Ramon Guerra stood in a clump of trees on a little hill on the east side of the Lavaca river, their horses tied behind them.

"Here comes the chuck wagon," Toombs said.

"Let it on through, we don't want to leave any sign that we're here," Kilgore said.

"One rider with the chuck wagon," Graves said, holding a spyglass up to his eye.

"I see 'im," Kilgore said. "That would be McCall."

"You'd better let me cross the river first," Cade said. "That way I can see how deep it is, and how swift the current is."

"Oh," Arabella said, apprehensively.

"What is it? What's wrong?"

"The water, it reminds me of the hurricane."

Cade chuckled. "It isn't nearly as swift as the water was that night, and I doubt that it's as deep as it was then. After I go across, I'll come back and help you get the wagon across. We'll make a second trip with the hoodlum wagon, so it'll be easier."

"All right," Arabella said.

Arabella and Maggie sat quietly in the seat of the wagon as they watched Cade approach the water's edge. He sat in his saddle for a moment, looking at the water, then he urged his horse on into it. He rode slowly toward the middle.

"Oh, good," Arabella said with a relieved smile. "Look, the water hasn't even gotten up to the horse's belly."

"He isn't all the way across yet," Maggie pointed out.

130

The two women watched as Cade rode all the way across, then, reaching the far side he turned around and rode back.

"It's not too deep, but it's deep enough to cause the wagon to want to float, so I'll cross with you."

Cade tied a rope around the axle, then rode alongside it, keeping tension on the rope. As he had suggested, the wagon tended to float and would have tried to go downstream had Cade not kept it straight with the rope. Once the team reached dry land on the other side of the river, they were able to pull the wagon up onto the bank with no problem. Cade unhooked one team of mules and went back for the cart.

"Go about a mile farther, set up your supper camp there," Cade said.

"Dinner," Arabella corrected.

"Dinner," Cade said with a smile. Then, bending down from the saddle, he gave Arabella a kiss before he re-crossed the river and rode back to meet up with the herd.

15

When Cade rejoined the herd, they were less than a mile from the river.

"How does it look?" Jeter asked. "If you remember last year the river had overflowed its banks, and we had to camp on this side for nearly a week."

"It doesn't look like it's going to cause us a problem," Cade replied.

"Good, we've had an easy start," Jeter said. "Goliath was a good choice for the lead bull; we've only had one little stampede that was easy to get under control, the men are happy and well fed—it would be great if we could go all the way to Abilene with nothing worse happenin'."

"Jeter, you know it's not going to be like that," Cade said. "I'll go over with the first group, you stay on this side of the river 'till we have them all across."

A few minutes later the herd approached the river and Goliath, hesitant to go into the water, stopped. Cade rode up to him and with prodding and urging, finally got him to commit himself. Once he was in the water and realized that there was no real danger, he hurried on across, with the rest of the herd coming along behind, each cow in his own, self-proscribed position.

As the herd continued across, there were periodic breaks so that, sometimes the cattle refused to enter the water, even though the cows ahead had done so. At such times the cowboys remaining on the east bank of the river would ride alongside the string, yelling, whistling, and waving their hats to keep them moving. There was a constant churning of the water as cattle and horses crossed the stream.

With all but about five or six hundred cattle across, only Jeter, Jeremiah Mudd, Muley Morris, GW Jones, and Troy Hastings, remained on the east side of the river. Cade had crossed the river, but he was just on the other side, observing the cattle as they exited the water.

Jeremiah Mudd who was on the right flank of the crossing herd, turned in his saddle to look toward a tree line that was on his side of the river, but about thirty yards north. He started toward it.

Jeter and the others didn't notice Mudd's departure, but Cade did, and he wondered what Mudd had seen. Then Mudd did a strange thing. He removed his hat, and waved it toward the trees.

Cade didn't know what that was about, but he didn't like the looks of it. Soon his concern was validated when he saw five mounted men suddenly burst from the trees. All five had pistols in their hands, and Cade worried for Mudd, until he saw that Mudd had joined them!

"Jeter!" Cade shouted, but because of the bawling cattle moving into the river, Cade's shout was unheard.

The five rustlers, six counting Mudd, began firing. Shooting their pistols was bad enough, in that it caused the cattle that had not yet crossed the river to turn and began running. Muley Morris, who was facing the charge, went down under the gunfire. That left only Jeter and the two boys to face the charging rustlers; three drovers who were caught totally unaware, to deal with six who had the advantage of shock and surprise.

Cade started to pull his pistol, but decided against it, choosing instead to snake his Henry from the saddle holster. Still on the opposite side of the river, Cade lifted one leg and hooked it around the saddle horn to give himself a stable platform. His first shot brought down Mudd, and jacking another round into the rifle he fired a second time, bringing down another man.

By now, Jeter was aware of what was going on, and he also began shooting, and a third and fourth man went down. The two remaining would-be rustlers, realizing now that they were alone, turned and galloped away. Cade had a thought about giving chase, but more than five hundred cows had been startled into a stampede and only he, Jeter, and the two youngest drovers were in position to go after them.

Cade crossed the river, then galloped after Jeter and the running cows. He passed the two young boys who were also in pursuit.

"Mr. McCall, what do we do?" Hastings shouted at him.

"We have to get in front of them!" Cade called back. "Follow me and do what I do!"

Cade knew from experience that there was really no way to stop a herd at full gallop. The only way to control them was to turn them.

He, Jeter, Troy, and GW reached the front of the stampeding cows, then began the effort to turn them. Waving hats, whooping and hollering finally had its effect, and gradually the front of this column began to react to their efforts. The galloping cattle were turned back on themselves.

This started the cattle into a large circle of bellowing cows, surrounded by a cloud of choking dust that hung in the air. This milling was kept up until finally the cattle, realizing that they weren't actually going anywhere, quit from exhaustion. Now, no longer running, they shuffled about slowly until Cade and the others were able to move them back into a manageable body. That established, they were able to bring the herd back the three quarters of a mile their mad dash had covered, until they were at the ford where the others had crossed.

When they got back, Cade saw that Finley and Campbell had come back across the river, and, while waiting, had also examined the five bodies that were scattered about.

"Rustlers?" Finley asked.

"Yeah. They killed Morris," Cade said

"Mudd too," Finley said.

"They didn't kill Mudd. I did," Cade said.

"You did?"

"If he hadn't killed him, I would have," Jeter said. "That son of a bitch was with the rustlers."

"He's probably the one who set the whole thing up," Cade said.

"Mr, McCall, you want me 'n Troy to go ahead 'n push the cows on across?" Jones asked.

"Yes, go ahead." Cade smiled. "You boys did a good job in stopping the stampede."

"What the hell happened?" Toombs asked. "I thought we had it all set up."

"Yeah, I did too," Kilgore replied. "We should 'a never trusted Mudd. Did you see how he come out there 'n started wavin' his hat at us?"

"Yeah, I seen that. I swear, I thought the son of a bitch had turned on us," Toombs said.

"Well, he same as did," Kilgore said. "Hell, he couldn't of done no worse if he had started yellin', 'there they are'."

"What do we do now?"

"I'm gettin' out of here. I don't know if they seen me close enough to know who I was or not, but I don't plan on stayin' around here no longer," Kilgore said.

"Where you goin'?"

"Anywhere but here."

"I'm goin' with you."

* * *

When they reached Gonzales, Cade had the herd held just outside of town, while he and Jeter took the bodies into town. Seeing two men leading five horses with bodies draped across the saddles, was enough to arouse the curiosity in all who saw them riding down the street. They rode straight to the sheriff's office.

"Who you got there?" Sheriff Gibson asked.

"Two of them I can identify for you...this one is Muley Morris, a good man, who was riding with our company. This is Jeremiah Mudd. He was riding with us too, but turns out he betrayed us, and threw in with the rustlers."

"The other three are the rustlers, I take it?" Sheriff Gibson asked.

"They are three of the rustlers, but that's not all of them."

"How many head did they steal?" the sheriff asked. "And what were the brands?"

"They didn't get any of them; we managed to stop them in time," Cade said.

"You plan to bury your two men here?"

"Yes, and I'll pay the expenses, for both of them. As far as these three," Cade nodded toward the rustlers, "I don't care what you do with them. You can throw 'em in the hog lot as far as I'm concerned."

"You'll find the undertaker down at the end of the street. Wayne Dowdy's the name. You can make arrangement for your two men, tell 'im the county'll pay for the other three."

"All right," Cade said.

With their initial morbid curiosity satisfied, most of the townspeople stood back and made no effort to interfere as Cade took the bodies down to the mortuary.

"This is Muley Morris," Cade said, identifying his rider to the undertaker.

"Surely he has more of a name than Muley."

"If he did, none of my men ever heard it. I think Muley
will be just fine to put on his marker. And I'd like your best
marker for him."

"Very good sir. And the other gentlemen?"

"This one is Jeremiah Mudd. I don't know any of the
other three, but I can tell you right now, the sons of bitches
aren't gentlemen. The sheriff said the county would bury
them. I'll pay for Mudd."

"And what kind of headstone would you like for Mr.
Mudd?"

"A pine board with his name on it is good enough."

"Poor Mr. Morris," Arabella said that evening as a sense
of melancholy shrouded the evening meal. "He was such a
nice man."

"*Oui,* but not Monsieur Mudd," Maggie added. "He
didn't have . . . ," she stopped in mid-sentence and looked at
Arabella for a translation. *"Personnalité agréable."*

"Agreeable personality," Arabella said.

"*Oui.* And I did not like the way he looked at us,"
Maggie said.

"Wait a minute," Cade said, "are you saying he bothered
you? Arabella, why didn't you tell me?"

"Oh, for heaven's sake, Cade, men have stared at me and
been forward around me for my entire life. I can't suddenly
come to you to handle situations I've dealt with since I was
thirteen years old."

Cade looked at her for a moment, then his expression
grew serious. "I guess you have at that."

The problems with rustlers seemed to be behind them, as the
herd proceeded north. They found adequate water and good
grazing and because those who lived along the trail were used
to seeing cattle drives, a brisk business had arisen between
the farmers and cattlemen. The farmers provided fresh pork,
chickens, ducks, eggs, milk, butter, cheese, fresh vegetables

and fruit to supplement the meals Arabella and Maggie were cooking. Sometimes the farmers wanted cash, but often they were willing to trade for a steer.

Waco, Texas:

When Amon Kilgore and Fred Toombs came over the rise, they saw cattle spread out before them. The herd had stopped for noon.

"Reckon they'll feed us?" Toombs asked.

"We'll soon find out," Kilgore said as he and Toombs rode around the herd, and approached the chuck wagon. There were three men squatting around the fire, eating their lunch. Not one of the three looked up. There were two more men standing by the drop down table at the back of the wagon. One had white hair and a white beard. He was wearing an apron that might have been white at one time, but now it was stained with the residue of a hundred or more cooked meals. The other man, small and wiry looking, was drinking coffee and he held an unerring stare at Kilgore and Toombs as they approached. He was wearing black trousers, a black shirt, and a low-crown black hat encircled with a silver band.

"Wantin' food?" the smaller man asked.

"Nothin' I'm not willin' to pay for," Kilgore replied.

The man nodded. "Good answer. Give 'em somethin' to eat, Squirrel."

"Pick up a plate," the cook said, pointing to a couple of tin plates.

"You the trail boss?" Kilgore asked the man in black.

"I am. Frazier's the name."

"Mr. Frazier, I couldn't help but notice as we was ridin' up, that you seem a little short-handed."

"I had two men that upped 'n left on me," Frazier said. "You two wouldn't be applyin' for a job, would you?"

"As a matter of fact, we are."

"You ever drove cattle before?"

"My name's Amon Kilgore," Kilgore replied, resolutely. "For the last two years I've been contractin' to take cows up to Kansas. Onliest thing is, they was so many cows kilt in the hurricane down in my neck of the woods, that there warn't but one herd a' goin' up this year."

"You was contractin' huh? 'N you rode as trail boss?"

"That I did."

"Yeah, well, here's the thing, Kilgore. This here herd is the Circle JMT, 'n I'm takin' it to Abilene for Mr. J. M. Truax, down San Antonio way. 'N it's already got a trail boss, 'n that trail boss is me, Silvanus O. Frazier. You two men would be nothin' but drovers, ridin' nighthawk 'n ridin' drag when your time come."

"You changin' out on drag? Most drives just put the newest ones on drag."

"See, that's what I'm talkin' about," Frazier said. "Already you're questionin' me."

Kilgore held his hands up, palms out. "No, no, I ain't questionin' you none at all. You're the trail boss, 'n I'm fine with that."

"All right. Soon as you eat, you can turn them two horses into the wrangler 'n pick out a couple new ones for yourselves. Looks to me like them horses has been rode pretty hard."

16

Twenty-one days after departing the LP Ranch the combined herd reached Ft. Worth. Leaving Boo Rollins in charge of the herd, Cade, Jeter, Arabella, and Maggie rode into town to replenish the supplies for the chuck wagon.

"We've come this far, and the men have worked so hard, I'm going to make a French Apple Tart," Maggie declared.

Jeter laughed.

"Why do you laugh? Do you think I should not do so?" Maggie asked.

"No, no, nothing like that," Jeter said, holding up his hands. "I was just laughing because in the whole history of cattle drives, I'll just bet nobody has ever made a French Apple Tart in a chuck wagon."

"Well then it will be a special treat," Arabella said as she and Maggie entered the Boaz and Ellis Mercantile.

While the women were busy, Cade and Jeter visited the sheriff.

"What can I do for you boys?" the sheriff asked.

"Tomorrow morning, we'll be bringing a herd through," Cade said. "We'll stay clear of the square if we can, but I just wanted to let you know."

"How many head?"

"Just over twenty-two hundred," Jeter said.

"Good and trail broke are they?"

"They've been on the trail for three weeks now; it's a pretty stable herd."

"What time you want to move 'em through?"

"I thought just before dawn breaks would be a pretty good time. It'll take a while to cross the Trinity River."

"Good idea. All right, either I, or my deputy will meet you down by the bluff. I expect you're on the prairie just south of town?"

"That's right," Cade said.

"You'd better put on a double watch down there," the sheriff said. "We've had some Indian trouble lately."

"We'll do it, and thanks for the information."

That evening, the chuck wagon was taken across the river and it was driven a little beyond Fort Worth. Cade intended to spend the night with the women, and he was lying under the wagon with his hands folded behind his head. Night had fallen, but because Arabella and Maggie were getting ready for the special treat they were making for the men, the two women had not yet come to bed. Cade was listening as they laughed and chatted in French while rolling out dough for the apple tarts. He would have to ask them if what they were talking about was so secret from him that they had to speak in French. He would be teasing of course; he liked the way the language rolled off their tongues, soft, and entrancing.

Then the seductive dialogue was interrupted by the jarring intrusion of a man's harsh voice. It wasn't a voice Cade recognized.

"What'd I tell you, Seth? Didn't I tell you I seen two women with this here chuck wagon?"

"Yeah," the other voice said. "But you didn't tell me they was both as purty as these two is."

Cade raised up, and peered through a crack in the canvas skirt that dropped down from the wagon bed. He saw two men, their eyes shining in the firelight, the lecherous gleam unmistakable.

"What can I do for you two gentlemen?" Arabella asked.

With pistol in hand, Cade crawled out from under the wagon on the opposite side from where the two men had confronted Arabella and Maggie.

"Damn, Carney, listen to her talk," Seth said. "She don't talk like no woman I've ever known."

"Isn't it a little late for you two men to be out?" Maggie asked.

By now Cade could see the faces of the two men as they moved closer to the fire. He remained just on the other side of the wagon, watching, but not yet showing himself.

"What me 'n this here fella want to know is, how come it is that you two women is cookin' for a cattle drive? Ought 'n there to be a man doin' this job?"

"Are you saying that you don't think women can cook?" Arabella asked.

"Nah, I ain't sayin' that," Seth said. "But seems to me like a couple o' purty women like you could make a lot more money if you'd just . . . Damn, Carney, I know why these two women is along! Hell, it's as plain as the nose on your face."

"What? What you talkin' about?" Carney asked.

"They're not a cookin', they're a' whorin'," Seth said. "Why, I bet these two has spread their legs for ever' man in the outfit."

"Yeah," Carney said. "That's it, ain't it, ladies? What I want to know is, if you're ready for some real men, on account of me 'n Seth here might like to have us a little fun."

"It's been most interesting talking to you gentlemen, but if you'll excuse us now, my friend and I have work to do. Please, run along," Arabella said.

"We ain't goin' nowhere 'till the two of you spread your legs for us," Carney said, as he began loosening his pants.

"Didn't you hear what the lady said?" Cade made his presence known by stepping out from behind the wagon.

"Where the hell did you come from?" Carney asked, as he turned toward Cade.

"I believe I heard my wife tell you to run along," Cade said.

"Your wife? Look Mister, we didn't know she was your wife. Iffen we would 'a know'd that, why we wouldn't a' come out here like we done."

"But you did come, and if I hadn't been here, you would have had your way with them. You're both a couple of low-life sons of bitches, and if I see either of you around these ladies again, I'll shoot you dead."

"You ain't got no right to talk to us like that," Seth complained.

Cade cocked his pistol, the action making a loud sound in the night.

"Yes, I do."

The two men exchanged anxious glances, as if trying to make up their minds whether or not to challenge the man who had confronted them. It took but a moment for them to decide, and turning away, they disappeared quickly into the darkness.

Maggie raised her eyebrows. "Maybe it is not good to be so close to a town."

"Maybe those two just came to get something to eat," Arabella said.

"I'm sure it was the smell that brought them," Cade said as he holstered his pistol. "Whatever it is you're cooking sure smells good."

"I think he's earned a taste, don't you, Magnolia?"

"*Oui*," Maggie replied with a smile, and from one of the tarts that was completed, she cut a slice and handed it to him.

"Damn!" Cade said after he took his first bite. "And to think that I was the one who tried to talk you ladies out of coming on this drive."

Cade left the two women and the chuck wagon before dawn the next morning, passing through Fort Worth in the early morning darkness. As he rode through the deserted street, he could smell the coffee and bacon of the early risers, and he was looking forward to getting the herd across the Trinity so he could have breakfast.

When he reached the prairie where the herd had spent the night, he was pleased to see all the drovers were up and moving.

"Are they ready for us?" Jeter asked.

"Yes, let's get them through so we can have breakfast," Cade replied.

"All right, boys, let's move 'em out!" Jeter called.

With whistles and shouts and with Goliath leading them on, the herd began moving. As the sheriff had promised, his deputy was at the river to guide them to the best place to cross.

Cade had intended to skirt the town to the east, but the spot the deputy chose for the fording was right in line with the main street of town. At first Cade started to tell Boo to turn the herd, but Fort Worth only had three or four businesses, a hotel, a blacksmith shop, and about twenty houses, so he decided it would cause less commotion to just continue as they were going. Then, when about a third of the cattle were committed, a woman came out of one the houses.

"Here!" she shouted. "Don't you let them cows break down my fence and trample my roses. Shoo! Shoo now!" she shouted, and she augmented her shout by waving her apron.

"No, ma'am, don't do that!" Cade shouted, but it was too late. The unexpected shouts of the woman and the waving of her apron was all that was needed to start the cattle running.

"Boo! Clear the street crossings, give the cattle room!" Cade shouted to the point man, and Rollins galloped ahead.

Cade rode up along one side of the herd while Jeter was on the other side.

"Get back, get back!" they shouted as the residents were awakened by the thunder of hooves.

The wild-eyed Longhorns began running pell-mell through the town weaving in and around the scattered houses. Cade saw the woman who had started the whole fiasco, standing on her porch, her apron in her hand. Her roses that were blooming profusely as they rambled along her fence were one of the only things in town that was left untouched.

It took a while for the herd to settle down, but by the time they reached the chuck wagon, they were under control. They let the cows graze as the first of the men began coming in for breakfast.

"Now that's a way to get your blood boiling," Art Finley said as he poured himself a cup of coffee.

"But did you see? Her roses weren't touched," Troy Hastings said as he took a bite of the tart Maggie had just given him.

"Hey, you reckon that woman uses that apron on her husband?" Mo Bender asked.

"Ha! I can just see her chasing him down the street," Art Finley said, and the others laughed.

"What are you talking about?" Arabella asked.

"Well, I'll tell you, ma'am. We're talkin' about a crazy woman that near' 'bout caused a big stampede," Troy said, then GW explained what had happened.

"I'm glad they didn't get away from us," Troy said. "I would've hated to have missed this breakfast, ma'am."

Maggie patted Troy on the cheek. "Thank you, Troy. Here, take an extra one."

"What about me?" GW said.

"Sorry, it's the last one," Maggie said as she began disassembling the camp.

She and Arabella had become quite proficient in the operation, as they loaded up the wagon and started due north. Cade and the others prodded the herd loose from what the cattle had thought was their bedding ground. As the herd moved slowly away, the riders eased into position around it. Pointers and drag riders resumed the same place each day, but swing and flank men often rotated. The herd plodded along, as slowly as a casual walk, and the drovers had to contend with boredom, for there was nothing more tedious than to ride along, looking out over the long, long line of two thousand head of cattle.

At noon, Cade gave the signal to push the herd off the trail, and no other order was necessary. The men knew exactly what to do. Half the crew, left point man, right swing, left flanker, and right drag rider, headed for the chuck wagon where Arabella and Maggie had dinner waiting. Even Arabella had surrendered her insistence that it be called lunch.

"I tell you what, Miz McCall, 'n Miss Maggie, I just don't believe there's ever been any other cowboys what's et as good on a trail drive as we've done on this here 'n," Petey Malone said.

After the first dinner shift had eaten, they saddled fresh horses, then went back out to be with the herd. Jeter had taken his dinner with the first shift, and now he rode up to Cade.

"You're a welcome sight," Cade said. "I was beginning to get hungry."

"Ha. As long as I've known you, Cade McCall, I've never known you not to be hungry."

When Cade rode up to the wagon, he saw Maggie in a conversation with Esteban Garcia. The two were standing behind the hoodlum wagon, out of earshot from the others.

"What are they talking about, so intently?" Cade asked.

"*Senor* Garcia is giving Magnolia directions on how to make tortillas." Arabella said. "Have you ever had them?"

"Sure, everybody who's ever been on a trail drive has had them, and when you spice up the *frijoles* . . ."

"But Cade, do *you* like them? Because if you don't, we won't fix them. *Tu es le patron*."

Cade laughed. "That's one French phrase I've learned, but even if I am the boss, it's good to fix something special for Tangora and Garcia. They're good men."

"*Vous êtes un homme bon*, Cade McCall. I knew you would say that."

Cade smiled. "I don't know what you said that time. . . but it sounded nice."

"She said you are a good man," Maggie said. "And she's right."

Seventy miles north of Ft. Worth, the Circle JMT herd had just crossed the Red River into Indian Territory.

"Peterson, you dumb sonofabitch!" Kilgore shouted at the youngest of the drovers. "What the hell was you tryin' to do back there, drown me?"

"You know I wasn't tryin' to drown you," Peterson answered.

"Then what the hell was you in my way, for?"

"I was ridin' where Mr. Frazier told me to ride."

"Yeah? Well when you're around me, you'll go where I tell you to go."

"You ain't my boss," Peterson said defiantly.

"I may not be your boss, but if you don't want your ass whupped, you'll damn sure do what I tell you to do."

Peterson glared at Kilgore, but he didn't respond. Instead he rode on, putting some distance between the two of them.

At supper that evening Frazier called Kilgore over to talk to him.

"I ain't goin' to yell at you, 'cause I don't believe in yellin' at any of my men, especially in front of the others,"

Frazier said. "But I want to know what you were getting onto young Peterson about."

"What the hell? Did that little bastard come complainin' to you?" Kilgore asked.

"He had a few words to say, yes," Frazier answered. "Now, I want to hear your side of it."

"I ain't got no side," Kilgore replied. "But I got a question for you. How come you, a trail boss, would get involved in ever' thing your drovers might say to one another. Don't we have no right to some privacy? Trail bosses is supposed to just see to it that the herd keeps on a' movin', you ain't supposed to get involved in ever' little thing that gets said. Leastwise, that ain't nothin' I ever done when I was trail boss."

"Yes, well, here's the truth of it, Kilgore. You ain't the trail boss of the Circle JMT herd, I am. Now, is it true that you threatened him?"

"The little bastard got in my way when we was comin' acrost the river, 'n almost crowded me offen my horse. I could'a drownded. But it depends on what you mean by threatenin' 'im. I didn't say I was goin' to shoot him, or nothin' like that. I just told 'im that if he done anythin' like that again, I'd whup his ass."

"I'll not have you takin' out on any of my men. Most especially young Peterson. For one thing, he's only fifteen years old. What sort of man are you, that you'd threaten a fifteen year old boy. And for another thing, Cal Peterson is Mr. Truax's nephew, and Truax is raisin' him, seein' as how his sister, the boy's mother, died a while back."

"All right, all right," Kilgore said. "I won't say nothin' more to the boy."

"See that you don't," Frazier ordered.

17

The combined herd, under McCall and Willis, was three days north of Fort Worth and the day had been hot and oppressive, without the slightest breeze. Not until they made camp that night did the sky become overcast.

"I don't like days like this," Cade said.

"You mean because it's so hot?" Arabella asked.

"It's more than that," Cade said. "Look."

Cade pointed to the western horizon where, in the fading light of day, flashes of sheet lightning lit up the clouds.

"Ahh, that's nothing," Jeter said. "That's so far away that we can't even hear the thunder."

"Nevertheless, I don't like it." Cade stood up and, drinking his coffee, looked out over the herd, now still for the night. "The cows don't like it either."

"You want to take a ride around the herd?" Jeter asked.

"I think it might be a good idea," Cade agreed. "Ian?"

"Aye?" the Scotsman answered.

"Have all the men keep their saddled horse right beside them tonight," Cade said.

"Is it difficulties ye'd be expectin' now?"

149

"I don't know. But I'd feel better if everyone is aware that we may be in for trouble tonight."

"Don't ye be worryin' none, for we'll be ready for anythin'," Ian replied.

Cade and Jeter rode together as they made a circle around the herd. Mo Bender and Esteban Garcia were riding nighthawk, circling the herd in opposite directions from each other so that they met twice on each revolution. Cade and Jeter overtook Garcia.

"How's the herd, Esteban?" Cade asked.

"Right now they are quiet, *Senor*, but I think they are a bit *nervioso*. They did not like this day, so hot, and no air."

"I can't say that I blame them. I didn't like it either," Cade replied.

As they were riding more quickly than Garcia, they met Bender on the other side of the herd.

"What ya'll doin' out here tonight?" Bender asked. "I ain't never known trail bosses to ride nighthawk."

"We're just taking a look around," Cade said.

On the western horizon, the sheet lightning seemed to be coming closer, close enough now that they could hear the distant rumble of thunder.

"I tell you what," Bender said, nodding toward the flashes that were now so frequent that they lit up the night. "That lightnin' oer there's got the cows kind 'a jumpy. I sure hope that don't come no closer."

"I hope so too, but I have a strong feeling that it's going to," Cade said.

Although, normally, the night brought some respite from the heat, this night was different. If anything, it grew even warmer and more stifling. Now the lightning was close enough that it was no longer broad sheets, but individual bolts could be seen streaking down from the heavens, and the thunder grew louder.

The last rumble awakened Goliath, and he got up and looked around, raising his nose as if smelling the approaching storm.

"Sing to them," Cade said.

Jeter chuckled. "You ain't never heard me sing, or you wouldn't say that. Lord, when I sing I sound like a heifer with a foot caught in a fence."

"We'll both sing," Cade suggested.

"What'll we sing?"

"I don't know. How about one of the songs we used to sing around the campfires during the war."

"Dixie?" Jeter suggested.

Cade laughed. "No, that song makes you want to get up and march. We need something soft and soothing."

"There's no way you can call my voice soft and soothing," Jeter said.

"How about *Lorena*? That's sort of soft song," Cade suggested.

"All right, you start it, I'll join in."

Cade began:

The years creep slowly by, Lorena,

Jeter joined in:

The snow is on the grass again
The sun's low down the sky, Lorena
The frost gleams where the flowers have been.

Despite the effort of the two men to calm the herd, Goliath had no intention of lying back down. Then another steer got up, and like Goliath, he too began sniffing nervously, expectantly. Other steers rose as well, and soon the entire herd was on its feet, and though they began to shuffle around, uneasily, there was no movement beyond that.

The night grew even darker, the lightning flashes closer, and the very air heavy with potency. And then, in a scene that could illustrate *Dante's Inferno,* on every tip of every horn of the steers, there appeared a ball of phosphorescent light.

"My God! Look at that!" Jeter said, awestruck by the sight. "Is that lightning?"

"No, I don't think so. It looks like St. Elmo's Fire," Cade replied.

"St. Elmo's Fire? What the hell is that?"

"I saw it when I was on the *Fremad.* Sometimes little balls of light, just like this, would form on the tops of the masts, or the tips of the spars. The old sailors said it's pretty common, but I must say I've never seen it like this."

The cattle, seeing the balls of light on the cows around them, became even more restless, and they began to move, not away from the bedding ground, but in a slow circle. Then, there was a sudden, huge spear of lightning, a great streak that came down so close to the herd that coinciding with the flash, the clap of thunder was as loud as the report of a firing cannon.

Within an instant the stampede started.

At the moment, there were only the four men around the herd, and they were unable to control it. But there was no need to shout the warning; the thunder from the storm was matched by the roar of over eight thousand hooves pounding across the ground. Those cowboys who had been sleeping beside saddled horses were up instantly, and they joined in pursuit of the stampeding herd.

Thunderbolts streaked down from the sky, one after another, until it was like man and beast were under an artillery barrage. The floodgates were opened, and the rain poured down in sheets, as strong as if they were standing under a waterfall. One moment the night would be so dark that Cade couldn't see beyond the head of his horse, and in the next instant a lightning flash would light the prairie in an unearthly glow of blue and yellow that would disclose the distant horizon. The flashing effect--now pitch blackness, then brilliant light--had a disorienting effect on the cowboys and the cattle.

The pursuing cowboys were trying to get ahead of the cattle who, at full gallop, could match the speed of the swiftest horse. But it was difficult to do so in the dark, because there was always the chance that the horse would step into an unseen hole, and throw its rider.

Cade felt a sense of loss and despair. He had brought the herd this far, was he to lose it now?

Then something totally unexpected happened. One of the cows let out a long, anxious bawl, calling for her calf, and it had the effect of bringing the galloping herd to a complete halt.

"What the hell just happened?" Jeter asked.

"I'm not sure," Cade said. Both he and Jeter had brought their horses to a halt and they sat in their saddles, looking out over the, now still herd.

"Cade," Ian said, riding up to the two men. "Should we try 'n take 'em back, or hold 'em here?"

Although it was still raining, the lightning had stopped.

"Let's stay here for the rest of the night," Cade said.

It was morning before they were able to return the herd to the camp, and there, Cade found an anxious Arabella and Maggie, worried about the men and the herd.

"I am so sorry, Cade," Arabella said. "But all of our fuel, the cow chips, the wood, it is all so wet that we could not get a fire started for breakfast, or even for coffee."

"Don't worry about it," Cade said with a reassuring smile. "It could've been much worse. We were very lucky."

Indian Territory:

Hey, Turner," Kilgore said. "You 'n Smith is ridin' drag today, ain't you?"

"Yeah," Turner said, disgustedly.

"How'd you two like me 'n Toombs to ride drag for you?"

"Wait a minute. Are you a' sayin' you *want* to eat all this dust?"

"Yeah, we'll do it."

"I don't understand. Why the hell would anybody in their right mind want to do that?" Turner asked.

"On account of I'm ridin' swing, right next to Carter, 'n the sonofabitch don't never shut up. At least, back here, nobody is always talkin' to you."

Turner laughed. "That's 'cause there's so much dust you can't hardly breathe neither."

"You'll trade places with us?"

"Yeah, only it ain't a trade. When it comes your time to ride drag again, we ain't a' tradin'."

"All right," Kilgore agreed.

Half an hour later, with the dust so thick that he couldn't be seen by anyone else, Kilgore left, leaving Toombs to ride drag alone. He rode off to find a Cherokee named Sam Feather, a man he had done business with the year before, when he had brought the Rocking D herd through.

"I can't get as many to you this year as I did last year," Kilgore said. "I ain't in charge."

"How many?" Feather asked.

"I think I can get you fifty head."

"I will take fifty."

"How much?"

"Five dollars a head," Feather said.

Kilgore nodded in agreement. "I'll bring them to Blackjack Coulee in a half hour."

Kilgore returned to the herd, and under the cover of the dust, cut out fifty head of cattle, just as they were passing Blackjack Coulee. He was met there by Sam Feather, who paid him two hundred fifty dollars for the delivery of the cows.

18

The Red River was considerably higher than it had been when Cade crossed it the year before. There was a ferry available to take the chuck wagon across, but it was going to be somewhat more difficult to get the cattle over. Goliath balked at the water's edge.

"I can get 'em across," GW said.

Cade thought back to another young cowboy, Andy Miller. Because of an accident at this very crossing, a once vibrant young man would never again be able to walk.

"I don't know, GW." He didn't want anything like that to happen again.

"I know I can do it, Mr. McCall, if you'll let me try."

He knew he was going to have to do something; he couldn't just leave the herd stranded.

"All right," Cade said, reluctantly, "and if you get Goliath started, there'll be fifty dollars for you."

"Yes, sir," GW said as a big smile crossed his face. He began looking around. "The ladies are already out of sight, aren't they?"

"They are, but why does that matter?" Cade asked.

"You'll see."

GW began stripping down to his underwear. "Here, Troy, bring these with you when you come across."

As the others watched, GW mounted his horse then rode up alongside Goliath, prodding him into the water. When the lead steer got into the water, a few of the others, reluctantly, began to follow. Within a few moments, the cattle began piling up at the edge of the water, because Goliath had stopped in mid-stream.

"That ain't a' goin' to work," Mo Bender said. "Them cows ain't goin' nowhere."

"Look at GW!" Troy said. "What's he doin'?"

The others watched as GW got off his horse, and stepped out onto the cattle, which were now crowded so close together that they resembled a raft of logs. Walking across their backs, he straddled Goliath, and urged him toward the far bank. Once the steer began moving, the other cattle began moving as well. GW rode Goliath on up the bank, then urged him to the side, out of the way of the herd, which was coming across in a steady stream. Here, he was able to transfer from the steer to his horse, which had swum across with the herd.

"Timmy, you think you can get the horses across?" Cade asked.

"Yes, sir. Uh, I don't have to take off my clothes do I?"

Cade laughed. "I expect that's up to you."

"I'll help you," Troy said, and the two took the horses upstream from the cattle. The horses didn't balk, and took to the river easily.

"All right, men, into the river with you," Cade said. "You don't plan to sit around and let these boys do all the work for you, do you?"

It took half an hour to cross the river and they did so without losing so much as one animal. About a mile beyond the river, with the sun gradually drying the cowboy's wet clothes,

Jeter pointed to three Indians who were sitting on horseback, observing the approaching herd.

"I wondered how long it would be before our friends contacted us," Jeter said.

"Friends? You mean you know them? There won't be no trouble?" GW asked.

"That depends on what you call trouble," Cade said with a little chuckle. "They represent the Choctaw nation. The one in the middle is Charles Pitchlynn. Like Jeter and me, he fought for the Confederacy during the war. The only difference was I was a sergeant, and Pitchlynn there, was a captain."

"A captain? Are you tellin' me there was Indians that was made officers?"

"This one was," Cade said. "And his pa was a colonel. Colonel Pitchllynn is some sort of bigwig in Washington now. Come with me."

Cade rode up to greet the three Indians. "Hello, Charles."

"Hello, Cade," Pitchllynn replied. "I wasn't sure I would see you with a herd this year. I heard about the hurricane you had down in Galveston."

"It was quite a storm," Cade said.

"With as many places reporting by telegraph as there are, you would think there would be a better system of warning those who are in the path of such storms," Pitchllynn said.

"Damn, I ain't never heard no injun talk like you do," GW said.

Pitchllynn looked at GW. "That's because I am from one of the five nations that you call, 'civilized', though I hasten to add that my people had a civilization on this continent for well over a thousand years before any of your people arrived. Tell me, Cade, who is this impressionable young man?"

"This is GW Jones, one of my cowboys," Cade said.

"Jones, you say? Clearly, that has to be an alias."

"No, I ain't no alias, I don't even know nobody named alias," GW said. "It's like Mr. McCall told you, my name is Jones."

Pitchllynn laughed.

"All right, Charles, what's it going to cost me to pass through, this year?"

"Twenty–five cents a head," the Indian replied.

"Ouch! It was only fifteen cents last year."

"Yes, and thirty cents a head when you reached the Cherokee nation. But William Ross and I have spoken, and we have come to an agreement. He is lowering his charge by five cents; we are increasing our charge by ten cents. It is only going to cost you a nickel more to get through the territories this year than it did last year. And, we will provide you with guides to help you find water and grazing."

"All right," Cade said, "that sounds like a fair enough deal to me. You can help with the head count. I think, at the moment, we have two thousand, one hundred eighty cows."

Pitchllynn closed his eyes as if in thought. "Five hundred and forty-five dollars," he said.

"Dayum! You ciphered that all up just in your head?" GW asked amazed by what he had heard.

"Yes," Pitchllynn replied. "Schooling is a wonderful thing, young man. You should get all of it you can."

"I suppose you saw my chuck wagon," Cade said. "You didn't give them any trouble, did you?"

"No, on the contrary, we had a wonderful conversation in French. I was surprised to see that you were using women as cooks. I must say, however, that the ladies were most delightful."

"One of them is my wife," Cade replied.

Pitchllynn smiled. "So, you married since you were here last year. Well, congratulations."

"Thank you." Cade drew some money from his saddlebag and began counting out the agreed upon price.

"By the way, I feel I must warn you to be on the lookout," Pithllynn said as he accepted the money.

"On the lookout for what?"

"There are some renegades, Comanche, mind you, not Choctaw nor Cherokee, who have been causing some trouble. Chief Ross and I have both put our police in pursuit of them, but so far they have managed to elude us."

"What would they do with the cattle, once they stole 'em?" GW asked. "Are they going to drive them up to market?"

"They aren't after cattle, young man," Pitchllynn said. "They're after horses. If they can steal ten or twenty of your horses, they can take them over to the western part of The Nations and sell or trade them."

"Thanks for the information," Cade said. "We'll keep our eyes open."

After they made camp that night, Petey Malone, Art Finley, and Boo Rollins began singing. When they started the drive, Muley Morris had been one of the singers, but since his death at the Lavaca River, in the aborted cattle raid, the three remaining singers had to carry on without him. It was obvious that they missed Muley's rich baritone voice, but the remaining three were good enough to provide entertainment for the others.

Cade and Arabella were sitting in their usual place, on a blanket against the wagon wheel, but Jeter and Maggie weren't sitting in their normal spots.

"What happened to Jeter and Maggie?" Cade asked.

"They're over there," Arabella said, pointing into the darkness.

"Over where? I don't see them."

Arabella laughed a throaty little laugh. "That's the whole point, silly. You aren't supposed to see them."

"Oh, are they . . . uh . . . ?" Cade started, but he didn't finish his question.

"You mean you don't know? I know you're very busy, but I can't believe you haven't noticed what's going on between Jeter and Magnolia."

Cade chuckled. "I'll be damn. I wonder if anything's going to come of it."

"Oh, Cade, why do you say such a thing? Jeter's not going to break Magnolia's heart, is he?"

"That's quite a question, isn't it? But, no, I know Jeter pretty well, and I don't think he has it in him to break a woman's heart."

With the Circle JMT Herd:

Wichita, Kansas was located just above where the Little Arkansas River joined the Arkansas River. The town, just recently incorporated, was ideally situated on the Chisholm Trail, eighty-five miles south of Abilene. The only thing the town lacked was a railhead, and the city fathers were actively wooing the railroad executives to bring a line through Wichita. In an attempt to make the town more respectable, the new mayor had ordered the U.S. Marshal to clamp down on the lawlessness that accompanied the drovers who came up the trail from Texas.

But those who made their living off the rowdiness that came with the cattle trade moved their establishments across the Arkansas and formed the community of Elgin. Within weeks, the town was wide open, with six saloons, one dance hall and three houses of prostitution. Elgin had no illusions of becoming respectable. They bragged that if someone was in need of the law, they could go to Wichita, but if they wanted to have fun, they should come to Elgin.

When Dan Frazier stopped his herd just south of Wichita, he gave half the men the night off to go into town. The other half were told they could go in the following night.

Night had fallen by the time Amon Kilgore and Fred Toombs rode out of camp. They didn't bother going into Wichita, but went straight to Elgin. The main street was a contrast of dark and light. Those few establishments that sold viable services—a mercantile, a blacksmith—were closed and dark, but the saloons were brightly lit and they splashed pools of light out onto the sidewalk and into the street. As the two men rode down the street, they would pass in and out of those pools of light so that if anyone saw them they would be seen, then unseen, then seen again. The footfalls of their horses made a hollow clumping sound, echoing back from the false-fronted buildings as they passed them by.

By the time they reached a saloon that seemed to be the most lively, the night was alive with a cacophony of sound: music from a tinny piano, a strumming guitar, an off-key vocalist, all augmented by the high-pitched laughter of women and the deep guffaw of men.

"What's it going to be?" Kilgore asked. "Whiskey or women?"

"Can't we get both at the same place?"

"Sure, you can get a woman at the saloon, but you have to buy 'em drinks, 'n it winds up costin' you more," Kilgore replied. "Why not just spend our money and take our pleasure? It seems to me like we only got one night, and I'd rather ride a whore I know than down a drink."

Toombs smiled. "Now you're a talkin'. Lead me to this here woman you know."

"Look behind you."

Toombs turned in the saddle. "Well I'll be damned. The Happy Cowboy." Toombs laughed. "Think the women in there can make us happy?"

"I guarantee you, they can."

The two men dismounted and tied off their horses at the hitching rack.

"How'd you come to know about this place, Amon?"

"I was by here last year," Kilgore said.

162

"Are they purty?"

"When you ain't seen a woman since Fort Worth, it don't make no difference what they look like," Kilgore said.

"Amon Kilgore!" a woman called out when the two men stepped inside. "I was hopin' you'd be back this year, but ain't you a little early?"

"Hello, Suzie," Kilgore said, as he reached out to squeeze her breast. "I ain't trail boss this year, so I'm just moseying up the trail. Ain't got a care in the world, cept thinkin' about you all the way."

Suzie laughed. "That's a big one. But ain't it sweet of you to say it."

Toombs cleared his throat.

"Oh, I forgot. This is my partner, Fred Toombs. Can you take care of him?"

"You want *me* to take care of him?" Suzie asked, a quizzical expression on her face.

"No, dammit, you know what I mean. Set him up with a good girl, but not quite as good as you. I don't want to hear him brag about his woman all the way to Abilene."

"There's no one that can top me," Suzie said. Then she laughed. "That is except you, Amon."

Kilgore took Suzie in his arms and swung her around. "Let's get these introductions over in a hurry."

"All right, all right. Girls, come over here!" Suzie called. "I've got somebody I want you to be nice to."

As the six young women approached, all were wearing practiced smiles. The smile on the face of one of the women fell away, and she stared at Toombs as intently as he was staring at her. Then the smile returned, not the wide, flirtatious smile, but a smile that was shy, and hesitant.

"Hello, Billy," the young woman said.

"Tennie," Toombs replied.

Kilgore looked over in surprise. "What the hell? I thought you'd never been through here before."

"I haven't."

"Then how is it that you 'n this whore know each other? And how'd she know your real name?"

"She's my sister," Toombs replied in a matter of fact voice.

19

Four days later, as the Circle JMT herd was stopped for lunch about twenty miles north of Wichita, Dan Frazier confronted Kilgore.

"We're short sixty-two cows since our last head count," Frazier said.

Kilgore took a bite of his biscuit that was left over from breakfast. "That happens," he said, nonchalantly.

"It doesn't happen to me," Frazier said.

"What do you mean, it don't happen to you? You just said you're short sixty-two cows."

"The point is, it's not normal," Frazier said. "Yeah, we lose a few cows now 'n then, but sixty-two? We've not had a stampede to speak of, nor a bad river crossing, but still we're sixty-two short. That's the biggest loss we've had since we left San Antone."

"What you tellin' me for?"

"I'm tellin' you 'cause I think, when you were ridin' drag, you just happened to cut some of 'em out."

Kilgore set his plate to one side. Gone was the nonchalant attitude.

"That ain't true. And even iffin it was true, what would I have did with the cows?"

"Sold them, I expect."

Kilgore stood up and with narrowed eyes, he pointed toward the trail boss. "Look here, Frazier, you got no proof me 'n Toombs did that."

Inexplicably, Frazier smiled. "I thought he might be in on it, thanks for tellin' me."

"Dammit, Frazier, I didn't say no such thing. 'N like I said, you got no proof."

"You don't understand, Kilgore. I ain't got time to be takin' you to court over this, so I don't need any proof. It's just enough that I *think* that's what you did, 'n so, that's why I'm firin' you. I'm firin' both of you."

Frazier reached into his pocket and pulled out two ten-dollar bills. "Here's the wages for both of you."

"Wages! Ten dollars apiece is that what you call wages? For all we've done for you?"

"You should count yourself lucky that I don't take both of you back to Wichita 'n turn you over to the marshal."

"We don't have to put up with this. You can't fire us, 'cause we quit. Come on Toombs, let's get out of here," Kilgore said.

Fifteen minutes later, with the two men a couple of miles south of the herd, Kilgore laughed out loud.

"A hunnert 'n twenty-five dollars apiece from the fifty head we stoled, 'n another ten from Frazier, I say we go back to Elgin 'n spend some real time at the Happy Cowboy."

Cade and the others were halfway through The Indian Territory and enjoying a supper of pinto beans and salt pork when the serenity of the quiet evening was broken by a loud, blood-curdling yell.

"Indians!" Ian Campbell shouted.

Boo Rollins grabbed the coffee pot and emptied its contents on the fire, extinguishing the flames. Cade, Jeter, and Rollins moved quickly to the chuck wagon, which was the closest place that offered any cover. "You two, inside the wagon!" Cade ordered Arabella and Maggie. "Get down between the flour and beans and keep out of sight."

The other drovers grabbed their guns and took what cover they could find, behind slight rises, or dips in the ground.

Because of the Indian shouts, it was virtuously impossible to know how many of them there were. Guns roared and dozens of muzzle flashes lit up the night. A bullet hit the iron rim of the chuck wagon, and a piece of it was shaved off. It carved a thin line in Cade's cheek, painful enough to get his attention, but he knew, at once, that it wasn't a serious wound.

One mounted Indian galloped toward them, leaning down low over the head of his horse. He was holding a rifle in one hand, apparently trying to get close enough to use it effectively. The Indian came close enough to be in pistol range, and Cade stepped out from around the corner of the wagon and shot him. The Indian fell from his horse. Cade shot two more times, and two more Indians fell.

A flaming arrow came arcing through the sky, then buried itself into the side of the chuck wagon. Cade ran around to the other side of the wagon and snatched the arrow down before the chuck wagon caught on fire, then he turned and shot the Indian who had launched the arrow.

"Mr. McCall, they're taking the horses!" Timmy Ponder yelled. Because the youth was the wrangler, he took a proprietary interest in all the mounts. And he started running toward the horses.

"No!" Jeter yelled. "Stay down, boy!"

One of the mounted Indians came galloping toward Ponder, leaning down with his war club raised. Just before the Indian was close enough to strike, Ponder raised his pistol and fired. The Indian went down.

There were actually two Indians who had approached the horses, and Cade, who had been using a pistol, set it aside and picked up his rifle. Jacking a shell into the chamber, he raised it to his shoulder, aimed at the second of the two Indians who had been trying to take the horses, and fired. The Indian tumbled from his horse.

The remaining Indians, realizing that the possibility of getting the horses was slim, turned and galloped away. The night, which but a moment before had been filled with gunfire, grew silent again.

"Cade, we'd better get some men out around the beeves," Boo Rollins said. "Tell the truth, I don't know why all this shootin' didn't get 'em with their tails in a roll before this."

"I've been thinking that myself," Cade replied. "Pick out a couple of the men and move on out. I'll check on the girls and then I'll make a turn, too."

The cattle, though made uneasy by the gunfire, had not stampeded. They were near water, and on good grass, so they seemed to be content.

After posting the nighthawks, Cade and the extra men returned to the wagon, where they were surprised to find that Arabella and Maggie had made coffee.

"This better not be Injun coffee," Jeter said as he squatted down on his haunches to pour a cup. Often when Indians came into a camp begging for food, a cook would pour hot water over the old grounds and serve it to them.

"Oh no," Maggie said flashing a smile at Jeter. "We made it fresh, and guess what else we made."

"I don't know, but I know it'll be good."

Maggie took out a bowl of small round balls of sourdough that had been fried in lard and then dipped in cinnamon and sugar. "These are for you."

"Hey!" Boo said slapping Jeter with his hat. "What about the rest of us?"

"Mr. Rollins, I didn't mean they were all for Jeter. I was just offering him the first one."

"Uh huh," Boo said nodding his head. "We know what's goin' on."

"I think Timmy should get an extra pastry for going after the Indians as bravely as he did. He was protecting the horses," Arabella said.

"How could you see that? I thought I told you to keep your head down," Cade scolded.

"I just raised one eye," Arabella replied with a smile.

"What do you mean brave? He was foolish, if you ask me, I think the boy should be givin' a whippin' for doin' somethin' so reckless that he could 'a got hisself kilt," Art Finley said.

"Well now, Mr. Finley, would you want to be tryin' that yourself?" Ponder asked. Though considerably younger, Timmy Ponder was every bit as large as Finley.

Boo Rollins laughed out loud. "What do you think about that, fellas? Timmy's done got hisself so full of piss 'n vinegar charging after them Indians, that now he's ready to take on the world."

"Here, Tim, have another one of these things," Cade said, as, with a smile, he tossed another pastry toward him.

"Yeah," Timmy said. "I'd rather eat one of these than fight, anyway."

Finley picked up the coffee pot and refilled the cups. "You're all right, boy," he said giving Timmy's shoulder a squeeze. "I'd ride to the river with you any day."

The next day, the Cherokee Chief William Ross met Cade to collect the fee that the US government sanctioned when cattle crossed the Nations. Cade told him about the attempted raid on the horses the night before and the chief, for an additional fee offered to provide half a dozen Indian police to ride along with Cade's herd all the way to the Kansas border. As a result of the protection furnished by the Cherokee Police, there were no further incidents while they were in The Nations.

Kanuna, the chief of the accompanying police, rode up to Cade just before they crossed into Kansas.

"We leave you now," he said. "We have no authority in Kansas."

"Thank you for your protection, Kanuna. We are most grateful."

Kanuna lifted his arm with palm out, nodded, then called to his men and exchanging the same greeting with the cowboys, they rode away.

"I'm glad they were with us," Arabella said.

"And it only cost an extra hundred dollars," Cade said with a little chuckle.

"Oh, I forgot about that. Cade, when will we reach another town?"

"We're about five days from Wichita."

Arabella wrinkled her nose. "Will it be that long?"

"Yes, unless we run into trouble, and then it will take longer," Cade said. "If you really need something, I think some men from Wichita have built a little trading post about a half-day from here . . . but you'll find about all they have are whiskey and tobacco. Is that what you're after?"

"You know better than that, Cade McCall," Arabella said.

"All right, I'll make you a deal. Do you have any dried peaches?"

"Of course I do."

"Then make us some fried peach pies and when we get to Wichita, you and Maggie will be the first ones into town."

Amon Kilgore and Fred Toombs had been in Elgin for the better part of three weeks. At first they were staying at the Happy Cowboy, but Suzie thought their continued presence was bad for business, so they took a room over the Trail's End Saloon. They slept till past noon every day, getting down to the faro table as soon as the dealer was opened for business.

"How much money we got left?" Toombs asked as they stepped out onto the stairway that led down to the street.

"Our stash is goin' down, but I feel it in my bones. Today we're gonna not only buck the tiger, we're gonna hog tie 'im," Kilgore said.

"Do you think maybe we ought to get into a poker game? I got good eyes. I can look over somebody's shoulder and let you know what he's got."

"That's the stupidest thing I've ever heard you say," Kilgore said. "You want to get us both killed?"

"Well, we've got to get some money somewhere, 'n I don't see any stage coaches to rob," Toombs said.

"Leave it to me. I'll come up with something."

When the two stepped inside the Trail's End, they stood for just a second to allow their eyes to adjust. Lanterns hanging from overhead wagon wheels emitted enough light to read by, though drifting clouds of tobacco smoke diffused the golden light.

"I'll be damn," Kilgore said. "I didn't expect to see him here."

"Who you talkin' about?"

"See that man standin' at the other end of the bar. His name's Sid Gorman, 'n me 'n him did some business a while back. This could get real interestin'."

With Kilgore in the lead, the two men went down to stand near Gorman.

"Who's this you got with you?" Gorman asked.

"The name is Toombs. Fred Toombs," Toombs replied. Smiling, he stuck out his hand but Gorman ignored it, instead lifting his glass to his mouth.

"I'm not in the cow business anymore," Gorman said. "So if you got some to sell, you're goin' to have to go someplace else."

"I ain't in the cow business no more neither," Kilgore replied. "That big hurricane down on the coast kilt a lot o' cows. So many cows drowned that most o' the cattlemen

171

wound up puttin' what few cows they had left all together to make a herd large enough to be worth movin' 'em up here. I tried to get the job bringin' the herd up, but old man Dennis didn't exactly give me what you would call a sterlin' recommendation."

For the first time, Gorman showed some emotion as he threw back his head and laughed. "And after all the cows you stole from him. Now ain't he an ungrateful son-of-a-bitch. But if you're not in the cow business, what in the hell are you doing in this hell hole?"

Kilgore didn't want to tell Gorman that he and Toombs had come up as mere drovers; it would have embarrassed him.

"Uh, Fred, here, has a sister lives nearby, 'n we come up to see her. You said you ain't in the cow business no more either. What kind of business brings you to Elgin?"

"Buffin'," Gorman replied.

"You? You're huntin' buffalo?"

"No, not me. Let some other slugs sleep under the stars for six to nine months to a year, not seein' another human being except some buck comin' for his hides and then his scalp."

"If you're not huntin' 'em, then what are you doing?" Kilgore asked.

"Makin' money. Some guy up north sent a load of dried up old hides to his brother in New York City, and what did that brother do, but tan the things and make 'em into leather belts? Now everybody wants more hides," Gorman said.

"Belts? Who needs that many belts?" Toombs asked. "Hell, most folks I know holds their pants up with galluses."

"Not that kind of belts," Gorman replied. "Belts for machinery. Back east there are more factories than you can count, and every one of them has a machine in it that needs a strong belt to turn the wheel to make the power. Turns out that buffalo hide makes real good leather for that. Yes sir, there's money to be made, and I intend to supply as many hides as I can buy from the suckers who'll sell 'em to me."

"Just how much money are you talkin' about?"

"Lots. A good shooter and a skinner could easily get a hundred hides a day, and right now that many would bring more than a hundred dollars a day."

"You're kiddin' me," Kilgore said.

"I'm not. You know the tale they tell about Bill Cody. They say he killed more than 4,000 buffs in eighteen months when he was working for the railroad and they were only taking the humps and the tongues. Maybe a haunch now and then when they felt like they wanted more meat. But they never took the hides, cause nobody knew what to do with them, except make a robe. But that's all changed now. The race is on to get as many hides as a man can get."

"This is very interesting," Kilgore said. "I might just find a way to do business with you again someday. Where you headin'?"

"I'm heading back to Texas, over toward the Panhandle. Everybody's huntin' in Kansas and Nebraska, but I figure the real getting' is going to be in the Territory and North Texas."

"Why do you think that?"

Gorman smiled. "Supply and demand, my friend. They're killin' buffalo like flies, but the government don't want white men killin' in the Territory, so that's where I plan to be."

20

Wichita, Kansas:

Where we gonna bed down?" Jeter asked as he caught up with Cade.

"I think we'll hold them a little north of Cowskin Creek," Cade replied. "The other day when we met Charley Singleton he told me the good folks of Wichita have put in a night herd law, but Cowskin Creek is exempt."

"Charley Singleton—he's the guy from the Circle Dot that was taken' their horses home?"

"That's him," Cade said.

"What's this night herd law?"

"It's Wichita's way of kowtowing to the farmers. They say they don't want cows running at large after dark—says it ruins their crops."

Jeter smiled. "Well, don't they?"

"I'd say they do, but if we have to pay to put 2,000 cows in pens, we'll find another route. Who needs Wichita anyway?"

"Cade McCall," Arabella said as she joined the two men. "You promised if Maggie and I made fried pies, we could go into Wichita."

"I did and you can. As far as finding a new route is concerned, we're talking about next year. It's too late to change now," Cade said. "Just for you we'll hold the herd here for an extra day."

"Good. That'll give the La Parra outfit time to get out of our way," Arabella said.

"The La Parra outfit. Listen to this girl," Jeter said. "You'd think she'd been born to the brand."

"You haven't mentioned the La Parra before," Cade said. "Have they been causing you trouble?"

"Not really. It's just that when Maggie and I are setting up the chuck, a lot of their cowboys seem to be out looking for strays. They're always coming in to camp asking for something we're cooking."

"Well I can't fault them for that. I'd take your cookin', or at least Maggie's, over any cookie on the range," Jeter said.

"If we don't get into Wichita for more supplies, it's going to be beans all the way to Abilene," Arabella said.

"Trying to bribe us, are you, Arabella?" Cade teased.

"Maybe," Arabella replied, with a wide, flirtatious smile.

The next morning, Cade and the two women left for Wichita. The town had a population of around three hundred, with an equal number of farmers in the outlying area. Because of this there was a good business district, and the recent attempt to corral the cowboy's carousing meant the saloons were respectable as well.

"This looks like the best place to get your groceries," Cade said as he stopped in front of Dagner's store.

"Who says we're after groceries," Maggie said as she jumped down from the chuck wagon.

"That better be what you want," Cade said. "Arabella says we'll be eating beans all the way to Abilene if we don't get a fresh supply."

"And that's true," Arabella said, "but any woman wants to go shopping."

"All right. You girls have a good time," Cade said as he lifted Arabella to the ground. "I'm going to go check in with the marshal and make sure Singleton was right about this night herd law."

Two men were standing in front of the *Vidette* office, having just picked up a newspaper.

"Did you see that?" Kilgore asked.

"Yeah," Toombs said. "That fella lifted the cookie out of the chuck wagon. That's strange."

"Ain't it though, but did you recognize that man?"

"Hell no. Am I supposed to know him?"

"I'd say. He cost us about five hundred head of cattle and killed four of our men."

"Cade McCall! So, that's what the son of a bitch looks like?"

"What do you say we go see what we can find in Dagner's place? There's somethin' odd about them two cooks, 'n I'd like to get a better look at em," Kilgore said.

When Arabella and Maggie came out of the store, they were both wearing new wide-brimmed straw hats that were tied on with ribbons.

"Just look what we have here," Cade said when he saw them. "Is this what you'd planned to buy all along?"

"No it's not, but they were so pretty, we just had to have them," Maggie said.

"They wouldn't look as good on any other women," a man standing beside Cade said.

"Oh, I forgot to introduce you, Marshal. This is my wife, Arabella Dupree and her friend, Magnolia Trudeau."

"It's McCall, Arabella McCall. My husband doesn't call my name that often."

The marshal laughed. "I know what you mean. Most people I know call me Marshal Walker, and it's just as well they don't know my first name."

"What is it? I'd like to know," Maggie said.

The marshal looked down. "It's Ina."

Maggie nodded her head. "I'll call you Marshal."

"I hope you don't have a reason to call him anything at all. After tomorrow we'll be out of here," Cade said to Arabella, then he turned to the marshal.

"I trust none of my boys gave you any trouble last night."

"None. We don't spend much time patrolling Elgin, and I expect that's where your drovers wound up."

"I expect so," Cade agreed.

"Well, now, just look who the cat drug in," a man said as he came out of the mercantile. "Cade McCall. How many cows have you lost for old man Dennis?"

"Not as many as you did, Kilgore," Cade said.

"Well you ain't got 'em to Abilene yet," Kilgore said. "You never can tell what might happen between here and there."

"You wouldn't be makin' a threat now, would you?"

"No, no threat. I'm just makin' conversation, is all."

"Marshal, I hope you're keeping an eye on these too," Cade said. He nodded toward Toombs. "I don't know this man, but I have to say that I don't think much of who he's chosen as a friend."

"They've been here for a few weeks, and except for a hand or two of poker that caused some sparks to fly, they haven't been any trouble."

"I'm glad to hear you're keeping your nose clean," Cade said. He turned back to Marshal Walker. "We'd like to stay here, but we've got to get back to the herd. My two cooks need to get supper ready before we head out tomorrow or my whole crew's going to mutiny."

"Cooks? These two women are your cooks?" Kilgore asked. "I thought you trailed with Ike Weldon."

Cade studied Kilgore for a while before he answered.

"Weldon's dead, and you knew that before we left Texas, or did you forget?"

"I guess I did," Kilgore said as he tipped his hat. "Ladies, have a nice drive to Abilene."

"There's something about those two," Arabella said as they walked away. "They were in the store when we were, and they kept watching us."

"Ma'am, I don't mean to be forward," the marshal said, "but any man would look at the two of you."

When the chuck wagon got back to the herd that night, Arabella and Maggie put together a delicious supper. They had fresh vegetables, eggs and ham, a meal everyone enjoyed, but the special treat was a fresh berry cobbler.

Breakfast the next morning was equally satisfying, and just before Arabella and Maggie left, Cade stepped up to talk to them.

"After we get the chuck wagon across the river, I want you to get well on out in front of us. I'm going to stay with the herd to make sure we don't have a repeat of what happened in Fort Worth when we're passing through Wichita."

"What about choosing a place to stop?" Arabella asked.

"You just keep moving north, and as soon as we clear Wichita, I'll catch up with you."

Cade turned to leave.

"Well, aren't you going to say it?" Arabella asked.

"Say what?" Cade replied, with fake ignorance.

"Cade McCall," Arabella complained.

Cade laughed. "I love you," he said.

"Well, now, would you lookie there," Toombs said. "Just like you said would happen. There's the chuck wagon all by its lonesome."

"You think I couldn't figure out what McCall would do bringin' his herd through town? Those fools down south might think they hired a jimdandy, but you just wait. They'll lose more cows with him than they ever did with me."

"Then why ain't we takin' the cows instead of goin' after the women?"

Kilgore shook his head. "I don't know why I put up with you. You heard McCall tell the marshal this here's his wife. You don't think he won't pay to get her back?"

"Oooooh!" Toombs rubbed his crotch. "But he don't have to get her too quick does he?"

The two riders overtook the chuck wagon and then passed it, one rider to either side. They rode no more than a few yards in front of the wagon, then they stopped and turned to face Arabella and Maggie. Arabella was driving, and she had to bring the mules to a halt.

"Hello, ladies," one of the two men said with a smile. Both Arabella and Maggie had seen such a smile before, and they knew it wasn't friendly.

"Sir, you are in our way," Maggie said.

"Yeah, we are, ain't we?"

"What do you want, Mr. Kilgore?" Arabella asked.

"I'm lookin' at what I want, Mrs. McCall."

Suddenly Arabella snapped the reins over the backs of the four-mule team, and, as if fired from a cannon, the team broke into an immediate gallop. Kilgore and Toombs had to jerk their horses around to get out of the way.

"What the hell?" Kilgore shouted as the wagon rumbled by them, with Arabella slapping the reins and shouting to encourage the team to run faster. The chuck wagon bounced and careened over the ground, with the pots and pans clanging as they moved back and forth.

For just a moment Kilgore and Toombs were glued to their saddles, startled by what they saw. Then Kilgore let out a shout.

"Well, don't just sit there! Get after them!"

The two men urged their horses into a gallop, and quickly overtook the wagon. Kilgore pulled his pistol.

"Stop!" he shouted. "Stop that wagon!"

Arabella paid no attention to him.

"Stop, damn you, or I'll shoot you dead!" Kilgore shouted, and even though he aimed the pistol at Arabella, she showed no intention of stopping.

Then, Kilgore got an idea, and instead of shooting Arabella, he raced up beside the lead mule on the near side, held the gun but inches from the animal's head, and pulled the trigger.

The mule went down in its traces, and that pulled the other mules down as well. With screams from Arabella and Maggie, the wagon turned over, then came apart, spilling utensils and foodstuffs. It lay there on its side, surrounded by a cloud of dust. The two wheels on the upper side were still turning.

The mules were braying in pain and fear. The two women were lying quietly, on the ground.

"Are they dead?" Toombs asked as he and Kilgore dismounted for a closer look.

"No, I don't think so."

Toombs pulled his pistol and stepped up to the mules, who were still braying in pain.

"What are you fixin' to do?" Kilgore asked.

"All of the mules, except for the one you kilt, has got broken legs," Toombs said. "I'm fixin' to shoot 'em."

"No, someone from the herd might hear the shootin'. Let's get these women picked up 'n get out of here."

21

With the herd across the river and safely through town, Cade rode over to Jeter.

"I'm going up to check on the chuck wagon," he said. "You can keep the herd moving."

"Ha! You're not foolin' me, Cade McCall. You're goin' to see if they got any sinkers left."

"You think so?" Cade replied with a smile.

"If they do, bring one back for me."

"All right," Cade promised as he rode away, urging his horse into a quick, ground eating lope. He had come about three miles when he saw the wagon.

"Oh, my God! No!" he said. It was more of a prayer than an oath, for he could see that both the chuck wagon and the hoodlum wagon were lying on their sides.

Slapping his legs against the sides of his animal, he pushed the horse into a gallop, covering the last quarter mile in just over half a minute. As he approached, he could hear the mules bellowing in pain.

"Arabella! Arabella, what happened?" he shouted as he swung down from the saddle and made a quick perusal of the scattered cooking utensils.

"Arabella?" he shouted, but the only response he received was the braying of the mules.

Cade pulled his pistol and stepped over to the mules. He hesitated but a moment, then shot the mules that were still alive. Seeing that one of the mules was already down, he formulated a hypothesis as to how the wagon was wrecked. The lead near mule must have stepped into a hole and gone down, that would have caused the others to go down, and that would have upset the wagon.

"Damn, Arabella, did you have them at a gallop? That's about the only way I could see one mule bringing down the others. Normally it would just be a quick, but easy stop of the wagon, and there'd be no danger." He spoke the words aloud, even though there was no one to hear him.

Then Cade took a closer look at the lead mule, and he saw what he had missed before. The lead mule had a bullet hole in its head, and it wasn't put there by Cade's pistol.

"What the hell happened here?" he asked, though even as he mouthed the words, he was getting a sicker, and sicker feeling. His curiosity changed, quickly, to fear.

Cade looked into both wagons, hoping to see them there, but he saw nothing. He got down on his hands and knees to make a closer examination of the two wagons, not only searching inside, but beneath them as well.

"Arabella!" he called again, this time in a loud enough voice to hear the ghostly return of the echo from a not too distant bluff.

"Arabella . . . Arabella . . . Arabella."

Now, on the verge of panic, he leaped into the saddle and made a large circle around the dead mules and wrecked wagons. He found nothing, but he didn't think that he would find anything because he was certain that the women, if they were still alive, would have started back toward Timmy and the horses.

On the other hand, there were no bodies, which meant, certainly, that they were still alive.

If so, where the hell were they?

Cade returned to the herd at a full gallop, and Jeter, seeing him come back in such a way, rode out to meet him.

"Cade, what is it? What's happened?"

"They're gone, Jeter! They're gone!"

"Who's gone? What are you talking about?"

"Arabella and Maggie! They're gone. The chuck wagon's been wrecked."

"And you didn't find them? Maybe they're just walking back to the herd."

"No, somebody took them. Jeter, it wasn't an accident. One of the mules was shot, that's what wrecked the wagon."

"Ian!" Jeter called. "You and Boo stay with the herd. Art, round up the others. We've got some searching to do."

"Mr. McCall, you'll need a fresh horse," Ponder suggested as he brought up one of the best horses.

"Thanks, Timmy."

Freshly mounted, Cade led the others back to the site of the overturned wagon. As Cade had done before, they looked inside, and under the wagon.

"Cade," Jeter said. "Look."

Jeter pointed to blood on the canvas. "Looks like somebody was hurt."

Cade examined the blood. "Thank God, it doesn't look like there's a lot of blood."

Elgin:

Tennie, we need help," Toombs said.

"What is it, Billy? What's wrong?"

"Kilgore and I found a couple of women. They've been hurt, and we need someplace to keep them."

"Why did you bring them here? Why not take them to Doc Dunaway on the other side of the river?"

"We can't do that."

"Why not?"

"Just believe me, we can't do that," Toombs said. "You're going to have to help me look after 'em."

"Where are they now?"

"Kilgore's got 'em out back."

"All right," Tennie said, letting out a long sigh. "We've got an empty room upstairs."

When Toombs went back outside he saw Kilgore with the two women. Arabella was conscious but Maggie wasn't. Maggie had a purple bruise on her forehead, and Arabella had dried blood on her forearm.

"Tennie has a place for them," Toombs said.

"Mrs. McCall can walk. Help me carry this one."

"What if she tries to escape?" Toombs asked.

Kilgore smiled, an evil grin. "If she even tries it," he nodded toward Arabella, "we'll kill this one."

"What is this place?" Arabella asked. "Is it a doctor's office? Magnolia needs a doctor."

"It's a whore house," Kilgore said, almost dismissively. "Grab her feet, Toombs, I'll get her shoulders." He turned to Arabella.

"You follow us, and if you try anything, or even if you tell one of the women in here what happened, we'll kill your friend."

Arabella followed them in through the back door, then up the stairs.

It was late afternoon by the time Cade and the others returned to the herd, empty handed.

"You didn't find them?" Boo asked.

"No," Jeter said. "Somebody took them."

"Took 'em? Any sign who done it?"

"If there was any sign, we sure rode over it while we were searching for 'em," Finley said.

"One o' the lads said ye found blood," Ian said.

"Yes, we did."

"Maybe some good Samaritans found 'em, and took 'em back to Wichita to the doctor," Boo suggested.

"I'd like to believe that," Cade replied as he switched his saddle to a fresh horse. "But one of the mules was shot. Whoever took them had nothing good in mind. I'm going into town."

"I'm going with you," Jeter said.

"Go ahead, we'll look after the herd," Boo offered.

Wichita.

It could have been Indians," Marshal Walker suggested. "Yesterday the Abernathys had three horses stolen, and their milk cow killed by Indians."

"Did they take anyone?" Cade asked.

"No, not this time. But a couple of years ago, a horde of savages came up here 'n raised hell. They raped 'n murdered fourteen women, burned a bunch of houses, destroyed eleven stage coaches, and then killed the drivers and passengers."

"You said, 'not this time' when I asked about what happened yesterday. What about the time you're talking about now? Did they take anyone?"

"They sure as hell did. They took four women and twenty-four children with 'em."

"I almost hate to ask this, but what happened to the women and children they took that time?"

"It was the middle of the winter, and two of the women and every one of the children wound up froze to death."

"Two of the women died? You said there were four."

"Yeah, well, about the only good thing that happened was Custer 'n his soldiers rescued two of the women at the Battle of Washita."

"But the women who didn't freeze to death, *were* rescued," Cade said, as if reassuring himself.

"They were.   We haven't heard anything about them takin' any women lately, but could be they took your wife and her friend. I was getting up a posse to go after the Indians that hit the Abernathy farm."

"Can you do that? I mean, as a city marshal, can you lead a posse out of town?"

"I'm not just a city marshal, Mr. McCall, I'm also the county sheriff. And the hot pursuit law allows me to cross the lines of my jurisdiction. If the Indians are out there, and if they have your wife and the other young lady, we can go after them."

"Then I'm going with you," Cade said.

"I am too," Jeter added.

"Jeter, there's no sense in both of us going. I think you should stay here, with the herd."

"For how long?"

"How long will you keep the posse out, Marshal?" Cade asked.

"No more than a week," Marshal Walker replied. "If we haven't found anything by then, we aren't likely to."

"If I'm not back within a week, take the herd on to Abilene," Cade said.

"All right. I'd like to go with you, but you're right, one of us needs to stay with the herd."

It took Marshal Walker no longer than an hour to raise a posse. Ten men, armed with weapons that ranged from a muzzle loading Springfield rifle, of the type carried by the soldiers of the Civil War, to breech loading carbines, to lever action repeating rifles, such as the Winchester, and Henry rifles. There was one double-barrel shotgun in the group.

Amon Kilgore, who had volunteered for the posse, was carrying a Sharps fifty-caliber buffalo gun.

"Damn, Kilgore, plannin' on takin' down a buff or two, are you?" Neil Lewis asked. Lewis, who owned the leather goods store, was armed with a Henry Repeating rifle.

"Not particularly," Kilgore replied. "But this baby," he tapped the rifle, "will bring down an injun from a quarter of a mile away."

"Amon, I thank you for going out with the posse," Cade said.

"I know we've had a few words pass between us in the past," Kilgore said. "But we're both from down on the coast, 'n that makes us neighbors. Seems to me like us neighbors should stick together."

They had been out for three days, and though they had found fresh sign, they hadn't encountered any Indians. They had just finished watering their horses when about ten Comanche came out of a thicket of trees toward them. The Comanche were coming at a full gallop, and they were whooping and screaming at the top of their voice. They were also firing at the posse, though because they were on the back of galloping horses, the shooting was inaccurate.

After their opening volley, the Indians turned around and retreated toward the thicket of trees from which they had come.

"After them, men!" Sheriff Walker shouted, but the words were barely out of his mouth before more than two dozen warriors reappeared to confront the posse. The Indians had drawn them into an ambush.

"This way!" Walker shouted, and he led the posse down into a shallow ravine, which got them out of the line of fire. They followed the ravine for a hundred yards or so, then when they rode back up to the top of the ridge that ran parallel with the ravine, found that they had flanked the Indians.

"Fire!" Walker shouted, and the posse fired as one, so that it sounded like one, sustained roar.

At least four Indians went down, and a couple more were hit. But the Indians, thinking that the posse would have to reload before firing again, turned toward them and charged, again filling the air with their war whoops.

"Those of you who don't have repeating rifles, engage with pistols!" Sheriff Walker shouted. "Engage at my command!"

Cade and the others who had repeating rifles jacked a round into the chamber, as the others drew their pistols. They waited until the Indians, many of whom were now brandishing war clubs, came to within pistol range.

"Now!" Walker shouted, and he punctuated his shout with a pistol shot. The Indian he had selected as his target tumbled from the saddle. The others of the posse blasted away, and the rapid fire decimated the Indians, but a chief began rallying his warriors. Cade took careful aim at the chief, then fired. The chief, who was holding his right arm over his head, waving his club as he exhorted the others, seemed to jerk in his saddle. Even from this distance, Cade could tell that the chief had an expression of disbelief on his face. The bullet hole in his chest was clearly visible, and after looking down at it for a moment, the chief fell from his horse.

That had the effect of demoralizing the rest of the Indians and, even though they still outnumbered the posse, not one of whom had even been wounded, the Comanche retreated.

Cade ran out to where many of the Indians now lay.

"McCall! McCall, get back here!" Walker shouted. "Some of them might still be alive!"

"I hope they are!" Cade called back.

The first Indian Cade reached was the chief that he had shot. The chief was still alive, though his breathing was labored. Cade knelt beside him, and offered the Indian a drink from his canteen.

"Why do you give me water?" the chief asked, his voice weak.

"Because you are dying an honorable death," Cade replied. "You fought well."

The Indian nodded. "I am Eagle Claw."

"Where are the women, Eagle Claw?" Cade asked.

"We do not bring women and children on a war party."

"I'm not talking about Comanche women and children. I'm asking about the two white women that you captured. Where are they?"

"We have no captive white women."

"Can you tell me these words truthfully? You are dying. Do you want to die with a lie on your tongue?"

"I tell you true. We have no white women," Eagle Claw replied.

22

On the whole, the posse's mission was deemed a success. Several of the offending Indians were killed, and the remaining Indians were driven out of the county.

"I doubt any of them redskin sons of bitches will come back to Sedgwick County," one of the posse members said.

"Not unless they're in a hurry to get to the happy hunting ground," another added, with a laugh.

The other members of the posse continued on in that vein, laughing and celebrating their operation. Cade didn't join in with the banter, because as far as he was concerned, it had been a complete failure. He had wanted, hoped, and even expected to either find Arabella and Maggie, or to at least get an idea as to what happened to them.

"I'm sorry Cade," Walker said when they returned to Wichita. "I wish we would have had better luck for you."

"I thank you for taking a posse out."

When Cade returned to the herd, the expression on his face said everything that needed to be said.

"You didn't find them," Jeter said.

"No."

190

"Well, at least you didn't find them dead."

"Walker said he would keep looking for them," Cade said. "How are the men?"

"They're concerned about Arabella and Maggie," Jeter said. "Oh, they've repaired the chuck wagon."

"Who's been doing the cooking?"

"Art Finley."

"Is he any good?"

"Well, given the circumstances, no one has complained," Jeter replied. "What do you want to do now?"

"I think we need to get the herd up to Abilene. I want to get them delivered, then I'm going back out to hunt for the women."

"I'll be coming with you," Jeter said.

"Good, I'll be glad to have you with me."

When Kilgore got back to the Happy Cowboy, Toombs was waiting for him.

"Anyone suspect anything?" Toombs asked.

Kilgore laughed. "That fool McCall still thinks it's injuns who took 'em. The sheriff does too."

Kilgore went up to the room where the two women had been held for the last week.

"All right, ladies, it's time to go," Kilgore said.

"Go where?" Arabella asked.

"Go wherever I tell you to go."

"Arabella, pourquoi sommes-nous ici? Je veux aller a la maison."

"What the hell did she just say?" Kilgore asked, angrily.

"She asked why we are here, and she said she wanted to go home."

"You want to say something, you say it in American, so's I can understand it."

"Ce que je ne comprends pas," Maggie replied.

"I said speak American!" Kilgore said, and he slapped her hard.

"Please, Mr. Kilgore! She said she doesn't understand what you are saying," Arabella pleaded.

"The hell she doesn't. I've heard her speak American."

"Yes, but the accident. She hit her head hard, and something has happened to her. She can speak and understand only French."

Kilgore smiled. "Good."

"Good? She's hurt, she needs to see a doctor. Why do you say that's good?"

"Because it means she ain't got sense enough to get away by herself, 'n you'll have to look after her. 'Cause it's like I said, Missy, if you run away, I'll kill her."

Cade and Jeter reached the railhead in Abilene with 2,175 of the 2,250 head of cattle they started with. They sold for $32.50 per head. After paying off the cowboys, and withholding their fees, they had sixty thousand dollars remaining, which they took to the Bank of Abilene.

"Yes, sir, may I help you gentlemen?" a bank teller asked, flashing an officious smile.

"We would like to arrange a wire transfer of some money," Cade said.

"Oh, well, our Mr. Broome handles such things," the teller said.

Broome was a very slender man with a closely cropped moustache under a small, narrow nose. So far during this cattle shipping season, he had arranged the transfer of over a million dollars, so he handled the procedure quickly and efficiently.

The money went directly to Linus Puckett, to be distributed by him to the other cattlemen who had contributed cows to make up the herd.

From the bank, Cade and Jeter went to the Western Union Office to send a telegram back to Puckett.

NET FUNDS OF SIXTY THOUSAND DOLLARS SENT TO YOU BY WIRE STOP JETER AND I HAVE

URGENT BUSINESS THAT PREVENTS OUR IMMEDIATE RETURN STOP BOO ROLLINS AND TIM PONDER TO RETURN HORSES STOP WILL REMAIN IN ABILENE UNTIL WE HEAR FROM YOU CADE McCALL.

From their own pockets, Cade and Jeter paid Boo Rollins and Tim Ponder an additional one hundred dollars apiece to take the horses back.

Except for Boo and Tim, who got underway almost immediately, the other cowboys spent a few days in Abilene to unwind from the long, hard drive.

While Cade and Jeter were waiting for the reply from Puckett, they decided to have their lunch at Waggy's Café, a place they knew well from previous visits to Abilene.

"Mr. McCall and Mr. Willis," an attractive, middle-aged woman said, greeting them with a smile. "Welcome back."

"Thank you, Mrs. Wagner."

"That isn't her name," a gray-haired, dignified man said. "Her name is Billingsly."

"George Billingsly," Cade said with a smile. "So you married her, did you? Good for you, and congratulations. How is your newspaper doing?"

"My newspaper, and this café, are doing very well, thanks to you."

Billingsly was talking about a previous visit to Abilene when Cade took on a man who was practically holding the town hostage. The despot was calling himself "Colonel" Dobson, but Cade recognized him as Albert Dolan, a man who had been in the Yankee prison, Camp Douglas with him. Dolan was not only not a colonel, he had also sold out his fellow prisoners, being the direct cause of the death of one of Cade's closest friends.

"Order what you will," Billingsly said. "Speaking for my wife, I can tell you it's on the house."

George and Millie Billingsly sat at the table with Cade and Jeter, visiting with them during the meal. The happy talk of their reunion changed, however, when Cade told them that his wife and another woman had been taken a few days ago.

"It has to be Indians," Billingsly said. "There have been two or three bands causing trouble, lately. Enough so that the army has been sending patrols out to chase them down."

As the discussion continued, a boy, wearing a hat with the words "Western Union" stepped into the café.

"Yes, Ronnie, are you looking for someone?" Millie asked, greeting the boy with a smile.

"Yes ma'am, I've got telegrams for Mr. McCall and Mr. Willis," Ronnie replied.

"Telegrams? You mean more than one?" Cade asked.

"Yes, sir, there's one for each of you," Ronnie said.

"I wonder what that's about?" Jeter asked. "Why would they send a telegram to each of us?"

"Only one way to find out," Cade replied as he gave the boy a fifty-cent piece.

"Thank you, sir!" Ronnie said with a wide smile over the more than generous tip.

Cade read the telegram.

MONEY ARRIVED STOP CATTLEMEN PLEASED WITH RESULT OF SALE STOP GOOD JOB

Smiling, Cade looked over at Jeter, but when he saw the expression on his friend's face, the smile disappeared.

"Jeter, what is it?"

"Pa," Jeter said, handing the telegram to Cade.

REGRET TO INFORM YOU TITUS HATLEY DEAD STOP MARY GRAVELY ILL AND ASKING FOR YOU.

"I've got to get back home," Jeter said. "I can't go out looking with you. I'm sorry."

"No need to apologize, Jeter. I understand. Of course you need to get back to Mary."

In calculating the fastest way to get back home, Jeter decided to take a train to St. Louis, then a riverboat to New Orleans and from there a steamship to Galveston.

"It'll take me a little over a week to get home," he said.

"Well, that's a lot faster than it took for us to get here," Cade replied. "I'm sorry about your Pa."

"He was a good man, taking me in like he did. I just hope Ma is still alive when I get there."

"I do too."

"And I hope you find Arabella and Maggie."

After telling Jeter goodbye, Cade returned to Wichita to speak with Marshal Walker.

"Sorry, Cade," Walker said. "I haven't heard a thing about the women."

"All right, thanks for trying," Cade replied, disappointed by the news. "I know you did everything you could."

"Would you like a suggestion?" Walker asked.

"It depends on what the suggestion is. If you're going to tell me to just go home and forget it, I'm sorry but I have no intention of doing that."

"That is my suggestion," Walker said. "Lots of young men like you have lost their wives."

"I'm going to continue to search for Arabella until I find her, or until I find out what happened to her."

Marshal Walker nodded. "I suppose if I were in your shoes, I'd be looking for her as well. All I can say is good luck."

Cade started his search by returning to where he had first seen the wrecked wagon. The wagon was gone, but he was able to locate where it had been by using triangulation between a copse of trees and a group of boulders. The accuracy of his positioning was validated by the remains of the four mules, their bones picked clean by vultures and wolves.

Dismounting, he stood there for a moment, trying to visualize what had happened, and which way they may have gone. South was Wichita, and north was Abilene. He was reasonably certain they didn't go in either of those directions.

That left east, and west. That he began his search by going west was an arbitrary decision.

After wandering around for nearly a month, Cade saw a building in front of him. It had been added on to so that lumber that appeared relatively fresh was next to weather-bleached, gray boards. A sign read:

MERRICK TRADING POST
GROCERIES, LIQUOR, GOODS
ROOMS, EATS
Merrick, Kansas

The inside of the store smelled of smoked meat, coffee beans, tobacco, and beer. A middle-aged woman, wearing a bonnet and an apron was sweeping the floor, and a man of approximately the same age was taking cans from a box and putting them on a shelf. Seeing that he had a customer, and still holding a can, he came over to greet him.

"Good afternoon," he said.

"Hello," Cade replied. He glanced at the can. "Peaches?"

"Yes, sir, Kinsett, the finest you can buy."

"I'll take that can right there," Cade said.

"Well, it'll save me having to put in on the shelf, won't it?" the man replied with a smile.

"This place is called Merrick? Reason I ask is I don't see Merrick anywhere on the map." Cade started to use his knife to open the peaches.

"I'm Jim Merrick, and this store is the town," he said. "Of course, I've not filed with Topeka, so this isn't an official town." Merrick reached for the can. "Here, no need for you to be usin' your knife. I've got a can opener."

"Thank you, Mr. Merrick. Cade McCall's the name."

Opening the can, Merrick handed the peaches to Cade who drank the juice, then fished the peach halves from the can with his fingers.

"Oh, that's good," he said. "I've had nothing but jerky and rabbit for the last month."

"Just wanderin' around, are you?"

"Actually, I'm looking for a couple of women."

"A couple?" Merrick chuckled. "Most men have a hard enough time handling just one."

"One of the women is my wife. They were taken by someone."

"Oh, I'm sorry. Please forgive the joke, I didn't know."

Cade explained finding the overturned wagon, and the mule that had been shot.

"It was Indians," Merrick said, resolutely. "There's a band of 'em right now that's causin' all kinds of hell. They say the one that's leadin' 'em is called Standing Bear. Him 'n his bunch raided a farm some north of here just two weeks ago, 'n they took two young girls with 'em."

"Two weeks ago? I hadn't heard anything about that. But then, I haven't seen anyone, so there's no way I could have heard. Do you have any idea where the Indians might be?"

"No idea at all. Somewhere here in Kansas? Out in Colorado? Maybe, could even be down in The Nations."

"That's a pretty broad area."

"Let me ask you, Mr. McCall. If you find Standing Bear 'n his bunch, what, exactly is it that you're plannin' on doin'?"

"I'll be getting my wife back."

"They say that Standin' Bear has at least thirty bucks followin' 'im. You plan to go after 'em alone, do you?"

"I'm going to get my wife back," Cade said resolutely. He didn't respond directly to Merrick's question.

23

Cade had been searching for Arabella and Maggie for two months without even turning up a lead, other than that Jim Merrick had given him a month earlier. He had to give up the search, at least temporarily, because the weather was getting colder, and he had no winter gear. He hadn't brought a coat with him, because he didn't expect to still be in Kansas this late in the year. He thought he would be back down to Jackson County, Texas by now. Instead, he headed for Wichita.

There was a chill in the air as he rode down Douglas Street, stopping in front of Marshal Walker's office. When he stepped inside, the first thing he did was step over to the little stove and hold his hands out over the heat.

"You look like you could use this," Marshal Walker said, handing him a cup of coffee.

"Yeah, thanks."

"No need to ask you if you've had any luck."

Cade took a swallow of coffee before he replied, then he wrapped his hands around the cup, enjoying the warmth. "I'm pretty sure my wife and Maggie were taken by Indians."

"What makes you think that? When you were with the posse and you shot Eagle Claw—didn't he tell you they didn't have any white women? Bein' as he was dyin', I tend to believe 'im."

"I believed him as well. But I talked to a store keep and a couple of farmers, and they told me about a band of Indians led by someone called Standing Bear."

"Standing Bear," Walker said. "Yeah, I got some information on him from the army at Fort Harker. He's been known to cause some trouble, lately. Do you know where he is?"

"No, but I pretty much know where he isn't. I've searched all of central Kansas. I don't have any idea where he is."

"I think you should go to Fort Harker."

"The army?"

"I told you how Custer and the 7th rescued those ladies at Washita."

"You're thinking I should ask Custer to help me?"

"Well, not Custer. The Seventh has gone to Kentucky. But rescuing white women, that's been somethin' the army's good at."

Fort Harker was used to protect the construction crews of the Kansas Pacific railway. But the railroad construction had nearly reached Denver, and there was little use for it now. As a result, only a company-sized unit remained, and it was under the command of Lieutenant Dwayne Metzger.

"I don't know," Metzger said. "You see how many men I've got here. My job is to close the post down. I have no authority to send men out into the field, looking for Indians."

"We won't be looking for Indians, Lieutenant, we'll be looking for my wife," Cade said.

"How long have you been looking for her?" Metzger asked.

"A little over two months."

Metzger shook his head. "I hate to tell you this, Mr. McCall, but if the Indians have had your wife for two months, the chances are likely that she isn't even alive anymore. And if she's alive then I don't see how you would ever want her back, because any decent woman would have killed herself by now."

Cade glared at the young lieutenant. "Were you in the war, lieutenant?"

"No, the war was over by the time I got my commission. But what does being in the war have to do with anything?"

"Because I killed a lot of men wearing the same uniform you are wearing. It's too damn bad you weren't one of them."

"What?" Metzger shouted, with spittle flying from his mouth. "Why would you say such a thing?"

"I don't appreciate what you said about my wife," Cade replied.

The lieutenant stared at Cade for a long moment, not with anger or challenge, but as someone who was totally unaware that his comment would be taken in such a way. Finally, he nodded.

"You're right, Mr. McCall, I apologize. I wasn't thinking when I made that remark. Please excuse me."

Cade said nothing, but he did nod his head once, not as much in forgiveness, as in a signal that he didn't intend to belabor the issue.

"If I were you, I would petition General Sully at Fort Dodge," Lieutenant Metzger said. "He has the authority to put an army in the field, and I can think of no more noble a purpose than the search for, and ultimate rescue of, a couple of white women being held by the savages."

"Fort Dodge, you say?"

"Yes, it's where the Santa Fe Trail crosses the Arkansas River. Fort Dodge has enough men to undertake such a mission."

"Thank you," Cade replied.

"And, Mr. McCall? Good luck to you. I hope you find your wife."

Again, Cade's only reaction to the Lieutenant was a nod.

By the time Cade reached Fort Dodge, Arabella and Maggie had been gone for more than three months. During the long ride from Fort Harker to Fort Dodge, he couldn't help but think about what Lieutenant Metzger had said. Not about him not wanting Arabella back, but whether or not she would still be alive.

Would Arabella be the kind of woman who would kill herself? Cade didn't have to ponder that question. He knew that she was too strong to commit suicide, and he also knew that she would never let Magnolia do it either.

Magnolia. Why had he thought of her in that name? She had always been Maggie to him.

Then he realized, with a sad smile, that he had thought of her in such a way, because that was what Arabella *always* called her. And he found comfort in anything that drew him closer, in spirit if not in body, to Arabella.

Cade passed through the gate leading into Fort Dodge, receiving only a cursory glance from the sentry at the gate. He started to ask where the post headquarters was, but he didn't have to. It was a small, but rather impressive looking building, shining white against the remaining buildings, all of which had grayed under the relentless blows of the sun.

Tying his horse off out front, he stepped inside where he was greeted by an enlisted clerk.

"Yes, sir, what do you need?"

"I would like to speak to the post commandant."

"Oh, well, I can't do that, but maybe the Sergeant Major will talk to you."

"All right, I'll start with the Sergeant Major."

Cade told his story to the Sergeant Major, then the adjutant, and finally, to the post commandant.

"I understand that your wife was taken by Indians," General Alfred Sully said, once the adjutant cleared the way for him.

"No, sir, I can't say that for certain," Cade said. "All I can say for certain is that the wagon she and another young woman were driving was wrecked, and we have found no trace of them."

"We?"

Cade went on to describe how Arabella and Magnolia were cooking for the herd that he was pushing up to Abilene from the Texas Coast. Cade also told what he had heard from Merrick and some of the area farmers, about a group of Indians with Standing Bear.

"Yes, I know Standing Bear," General Sully replied, with a nod of his head. "He's half Comanche and half Cheyenne, and doesn't get along with either. He has a band made up of outcasts from both tribes, and given some of the recent depredations he has committed I would say that it's a good chance that he may well be the one who took the women. What have you done, so far, by way of looking for them?"

"Sheriff Walker, in Sedgwick County formed a posse and I went with him. We encountered a small band of Indians..."

"Yes, Sheriff Walker sent his report on to me," General Sully said. "I believe it was Eagle Claw and a small band. It was good that you killed him."

"Yes, I suppose so."

"You suppose so? What an odd response."

Cade thought of the Indian chief, dying with honor, relieving his mind that he had had nothing to do with the disappearance of Arabella and Magnolia.

"What I meant was we didn't find my wife with Eagle Claw's band. And since I left Sheriff Walker, I've spent the last two and a half, almost three, months looking for them on my own. So far, I'm sorry to say, I haven't found so much as one hint as to where they might be or even what happened to them. Sheriff Walker is the one who suggested that I ask the army for help. I went to Fort Harker, but Lieutenant Metzger said he wasn't in a position to help. He's the one who suggested that I come see you."

"Mr. McCall, I hate to say this, but have you considered that your wife and her friend might be dead?"

"Yes, of course I have, and Metzger raised that same point with me."

"He was right, you know. Indians will take the young and raise them as their own. But grown men and women don't fare as well. They generally kill the men, immediately, and they'll keep the women alive only long enough to use them; then they'll kill them as well."

"I've not only considered that, I've dwelled upon it."

"But you still want to search for them?"

"Yes."

General Sully pulled upon his chin whiskers as he studied Cade. "Well, I can't say as I blame you. I'll tell you what. I'll send an augmented patrol out looking for them."

"I was hoping you'd do that. I'd very much like to go with the patrol."

General Sully shook his head. "Impossible. We can't take a civilian with us."

"Then I'll follow along behind your patrol," Cade insisted.

Sully chuckled. "You would do that, wouldn't you?"

"Yes, sir, I would."

"I've got an idea, if you are amenable to it."

"I don't intend to join the army," Cade said. "Right now I have only one purpose in life, and that is to find my wife, or barring that, at least to find out what happened to her."

"You won't exactly be joining the army, but you will be a part of the Table of Organization. How would you like to be a civilian scout, assigned to the Eleventh Cavalry?"

"How long would I have to serve in that position?" Cade asked.

"Only as long as you want to."

Cade smiled. "I never thought I'd be a part of the Yankee army, but sign me up."

"Your pay is twenty-one dollars a month," General Sully said. "Not much, I know, but consider that even the most senior of the troopers makes only sixteen dollars a month."

"The money isn't important," Cade said.

"I had a feeling it wouldn't be. Since the army won't be furnishing any of your supplies, you might check in with Jesse Crane over at the Sutler store. He can give you an idea of what you'll need."

"So, you're signing on as a scout, are you?" Crane asked.

"Yes. General Sully said that you'd be able to sell me what I need for the expedition."

"More than happy to, sonny, more than happy to," Crane said. "We'd better start by getting you into some different duds. Most scouts like to wear buckskin trousers and shirts. They don't wear out, and they're pretty good about keeping the rain off. But what you really need for that is a good poncho, and I can sell you that, too."

"I appreciate that."

"And, with winter coming on, you'll want something warm. A buffalo coat, perhaps."

"I definitely want something to keep me warm."

"You got 'nything you can use as a pack animal?" Crane asked.

"No."

"You'd better buy one. Even though you're a scout, you're still a civilian, and the trains won't be able to carry any of your gear for you."

"Where can I buy an extra horse?"

Crane shook his head. "You don't want a horse; you want a mule, 'n I can get that for you as well."

Half an hour later, Cade had bought two buckskin outfits, a buffalo robe, a knife, one hundred rounds of .44-40 ammunition for his Winchester, and one hundred .45 caliber rounds for his pistol.

"I can give you a shelter half, if you can find a soldier to buddy up with when you pitch your tent," Crane said. "But truth is, most of the soldiers has already got 'em a buddy, so unless you buy both halves, you won't have no way to keep yourself dry if it rains at night while you're in bivouac."

"Then give me both halves," Cade said.

Cade was just paying for his purchases when a lieutenant came into the Sutler Store.

"Mr. McCall?"

"Yes, I'm McCall," Cade replied.

"I'm Lieutenant Chambers. I'm in command of D Troop. We will be making the patrol."

"It's nice meeting you," Cade replied. "When do we leave?"

"We'll get underway at one o'clock this afternoon. Please repair to the parade ground at that time."

"I'll report at one o'clock."

"We will form up there," Chambers said. "You, being a scout, will not be a part of the formation, but you should be mounted, and ready to leave when we leave."

"All right," Cade agreed.

24

When Cade reported to the parade ground at the appointed time he saw several men standing by their horses, but not mounted. Much of the post had turned out to watch their departure, including the women and children who stood to one side. He was surprised to see the band was there as well.

A young second lieutenant approached him. "Mr. McCall?"

"Yes?"

"Compliments of General Sully, sir. He invites you to join him at the flag pole."

"Thank you." Cade started to follow him.

"Oh, and bring your horse and your mule, sir," the lieutenant said.

Deciding not to walk when he could ride, Cade mounted his horse, and leading the mule, followed the lieutenant.

"Dismount, Mr. McCall," General Sully said in a friendly tone. "Private Lemon will hold your mount and pack mule until Lieutenant Chambers departs, then you can join them. I thought, in the meantime, you might like to watch the duty formation with me."

"Thank you, Colonel."

A young private came to take Cade's horse and mule, then stood back as the company prepared to get underway. There were several troopers standing out in the parade ground visiting with each other. Lieutenant Chambers came riding up to the parade ground then, while still mounted, he addressed the assembled soldiers.

"D Troop, to horse!" Lieutenant Chambers commanded, and quickly the troopers fell into a formation, with every soldier standing by his horse.

"Prepare to mount," he ordered. Then, "Mount."

As one, the men mounted.

The formation consisted of two ranks of men, all of them facing toward Chambers, and the general. Chambers turned to face the general, then saluted.

"Sir, D Troop is mounted and ready to depart!" he shouted.

General Sully returned Chambers' salute.

"Very good, Mr. Chambers. Carry on with the patrol!"

Chambers turned back to the formation. "First Sergeant, post!"

A soldier with three stripes and a diamond on his arm moved into the front of the patrol. There was something about him that seemed familiar to Cade, but he wasn't close enough to see his face that clearly, and of course, he was in no position to improve his vantage point.

"D Troop, left by twos, forward, ho!" Lieutenant Chambers called.

At his command, the troop began moving out at a swift trot, while the band played *The Girl I Left Behind Me.*

"All right, Mr. McCall. It's time for you to join them," General Sully said.

Cade started toward his horse but he didn't have to, as Private Lemon was right there with it. Mounting, he considered saluting the general, but, as he wasn't in the army, he didn't know whether he should or not. Instead, he just nodded, then turned to follow the troop, which was already passing through the gate. He fell in with the trains detail, which consisted of a sergeant and four privates, each private leading two pack mules.

They had been on the march for a little over an hour, when they stopped for their first rest. Cade was adjusting the pack on his mule when someone came up behind him.

"Hello, Sergeant McCall. I thought you were killed at Franklin."

Surprised to hear a voice he recognized, Cade turned. "Captain Hanner!" he said.

With a chuckle, Hanner pointed to the stripes on his sleeve. "It's Sergeant Hanner now," he said. "The Yankee army wasn't all that interested in granting commissions to former Confederate officers."

Like Cade, Hanner had been part of the 33rd Tennessee during the war. And this was the NCO who had been vaguely familiar to him as the patrol was forming up on the parade ground.

"What happened to you?" Hanner said. "I can see that you weren't killed."

Cade explained how he had finished out the war as a prisoner at Camp Douglas.

"What are you doing out here?" Hanner asked. "I thought you and your girl were planning on settling down on that farm outside Clarksville. What was her name? Melinda?"

"Melinda did settle down on that farm. With my brother," Cade said.

"Oh?"

"You aren't the only one who thought I was dead."

"Wait a minute, I was told we would be looking for a couple of white women."

"Yes. My wife, Arabella, and her friend, Magnolia."

Hanner put his hand on Cade's shoulder. "I hope we find them, McCall."

"Thanks."

"First Sergeant, assemble the men!" Chambers ordered.

"All right men, mount up!" Sergeant Hanner called.

The augmented patrol followed sign and interviewed farmers and store keeps. As the fall dragged on the weather grew cooler, but the bitter cold held off.

Cade didn't mind the days, so much. They were riding, looking for sign, and asking questions of everyone they came across. It was the nighttime that he didn't like. He lay in his tent, awake, long after he should have been asleep, thinking about Arabella, and wondering what she was going through. Was she still alive? If so, had she given up all hope of ever being found?

They had been out for three weeks when they came across a store that, by its very remoteness, was able to survive because there was no competition for the scattered farmers, buffalo hunters, and occasional Indians who came by to trade.

"Yeah, I've done business with Standing Bear," Maynard Logan, the owner of the trading post said.

"You do business with savages?" Lieutenant Chambers asked.

"Lieutenant, if you've rode out here, you know there ain't no law or soldiers within fifty miles. The only way I can stay alive is to treat ever' one the same, 'n that means farmers, ranchers, buffalo hunters, outlaws, 'n injuns. 'N one of them injuns I've done business with is Standin' Bear."

"Did he have any women with him?" Cade asked, anxiously.

"Yeah, he had women," Logan said. "He's travelin' with about 40 warriors, 'n prob'ly 20 or more squaws, plus a passel of little injun brats."

"Were there any white women with him?" Cade asked.

"White women? Yeah, now that I recall, they was two white women in amongst the squaws."

"Where is he now?" Cade asked, anxiously. "Where did Standing Bear go?"

"I can tell you where he went. But, that ought to be worth somethin', shouldn't it?"

"I'll give you one hundred dollars for the information," Cade said.

Logan smiled and held out his hand. Not until Cade gave him five twenty-dollar bills did he speak.

"I heard some of 'em talkin'. They plan to make a winter camp down on Bear Creek. That's about fifty miles from here, in Hamilton County."

They reached Bear Creek, in the extreme southwest part of Kansas, by midafternoon the next day. Here, all signs indicated that they were very near Standing Bear and his band.

"Men," Chambers said, standing in the stirrups to address the platoon. "We are going to ride up the creek bed. We will start at a canter; continue the canter for ten minutes, then slow to a trot. Above all, keep it closed up, and keep moving!"

"Sir, if I may suggest, it would be better to ride along the ridge line, following the creek bed," Sergeant Hanner said.

"Thank you for your suggestion, First Sergeant, but we will follow the creek bed."

"With all due respect, Lieutenant, we've seen too much sign. It's for sure and certain that Standing Bear is here. I just don't think that it would be such a good idea to expose ourselves like that."

"You may have been a captain in the Confederacy, First Sergeant Hanner, but here you are an enlisted man, and that means you are subject to my orders. We can move much faster by staying in the creek bed than we can by riding up on the ridge line where we will constantly be traversing gullies."

"Yes, sir," Hanner replied.

"Forward, ho!" Chambers ordered, and the platoon started forward at the canter.

"Lieutenant," Sergeant Hanner called about half-an-hour later. "Look up ahead. See how the walls close in on the creek bed like that? Once we get in there, it will be too narrow for maneuvering. I recommend that we leave this creek bed and take the high ground, just until we are through that restricted canyon ahead."

"You heard my orders, First Sergeant. We will continue as before."

"Lieutenant, I think you should listen to Cap . . . that is, Sergeant Hanner," Cade said. One of the soldiers with the train had offered to take Cade's mule in tow, which freed him to ride up with the head of the troop.

"Mr. McCall, it is enough that I have to put up with insubordination from an NCO, I will *not* put up with it from a civilian scout. We will continue as before."

They were half-way through the narrow canyon and Cade was beginning to hope they might make it all the way without incident, when there was a sudden shout, followed by a horse whinnying in pain.

"Injuns!" someone shouted, and looking around, Cade saw a cloud of arrows raining down upon them. Most of the arrows clattered off the steep rocky walls on either side of them, but from the shouts and groans of fear and pain, Cade knew that at least some of them had found their mark.

"Dismount! Dismount!" Chambers ordered.

"Lieutenant, no! We can't dismount! We're in a confined area! We've got to get out of here!" Hanner shouted.

"First Sergeant Hanner, quit questioning my commands!" Chambers screamed.

The patrol was made up of seasoned cavalrymen who knew that the moment a body of cavalry dismounted, it would lose one-fourth of its effective fighting force by virtue of the fact that every fourth man was detailed to hold the horses of the other three. They also knew that if they dismounted here, they would be sitting ducks for the Indians up on the ridge line. But they were, above all, soldiers, and they had been given their orders. They dismounted.

The arrows continued to rain down and more men were hit.

"Lieutenant, we're getting slaughtered here!" one of the troopers shouted.

"Lieutenant Chambers, we must remount!" Hanner shouted.

At that moment one of the troopers holding the horses was hit. He was right in front of Chambers, and seeing him, Chambers panicked. He opened his mouth, but was unable to speak.

"Mount up!" Hanner called, assuming command.

Even as Hanner was giving the command, Chambers was brought down, not by an arrow, but by a rifle shot, for now the Indians who were armed with rifles had joined in the fray. Cade looked at the fallen lieutenant and saw that the bullet had struck him in the forehead, killing him instantly.

"Column of twos, forward at a gallop!" Hanner shouted, leading the men out of the narrow restriction.

After about a hundred yards, they reached a part of the gully that had sloping sides so that they were able to exit quite easily. Very quickly, they were up on top of the ridge, and at the same level as the Indians.

"Now!" Hanner shouted to the men. "Skirmish line front! Charge! Charge the bastards!"

At this point the situation changed, and the advantage belonged to the cavalry, for the Indians were not only dismounted, they were surprised by the sudden and unexpected counter-attack.

The troopers began firing and several of the Indians went down. The remaining Indians began to run. The cavalry charged at a full gallop until, finally, they reached a very deep cross-gully with walls that were much too steep for the horses to go down. Here, the Indians managed to slip into crevices and behind rocks as they scrambled down the canyon face to the floor.

Once on the gully floor, the Indians were able to find draws and off-shoot canyons which allowed them to get away. The soldiers were still firing, even though by now all the Indians had managed to scramble to safety, and there were no real targets.

"Cease fire, cease fire! You're wasting ammunition!" Hanner shouted.

The firing fell off raggedly, with the last few shots echoing back from the gully walls. By now all the Indians were gone and there was only the sound of a sighing wind.

Hanner looked around at the soldiers who were with him. "Did we lose any more men?" he asked.

"Not since the first volleys, First Sergeant," one of the troopers replied.

"All right, we'll go back down and recover the wounded and bury the dead," Hanner said.

"First Sergeant, they's some squaws over there," one of the soldiers said.

Looking in the direction the trooper had pointed, Cade saw a pitiful collection of women and children, gathered in a little group.

"Damn, they's a couple of white women with 'em!" someone shouted.

Without hesitation, Cade remounted and rode toward the gathering of women and children. They drew back in fear as he approached. At first glance, he didn't see anyone who looked white, all were dressed alike. But of course, this long after their capture it was very unlikely that Arabella or Magnolia would be wearing the same thing they were wearing when they were captured.

"Arabella! Arabella!" he shouted, excitedly. "Arabella, it's me, Cade!"

Nobody responded, and he went through them, pulling away their blankets, until he found the two white women. He didn't recognize either one of them.

"Who are you?" he asked.

One of the women responded in a language that Cade didn't recognize.

"She's speaking Cheyenne," Hanner said, joining him. "Your wife?"

Cade shook his head. "No. I don't know them."

"We aren't going to hurt you," Hanner said. "We're going to take you back to your families."

"We have no family," one of the women said.

"You can speak English!" Cade said, excitedly.

"Yes."

"I'm looking for two white women. Arabella and Magnolia. Do you know anything about them?"

The two women looked at each other and shook their heads.

"No," the one who had been speaking said. "We have heard nothing about two more white women."

25

Fort Dodge, KS

What will happen to the two white women we brought back?" Cade asked General Sully.

"A couple of our Fort Dodge families have offered to take them in until they are acclimated into white society again. It's going to take them a while to be able to live with themselves, they have such a strong sense of guilt," General Sully replied.

"They have nothing to feel guilty about," Cade said, resolutely.

The general started to reply, but checked his words. "You're right of course, it was no more their fault than it is the fault of whatever your wife has gone through. Sergeant Hanner, and the others, had high praise for you on this scout. If you would like to stay on, the army would be happy to have you."

"Thank you, General, for giving me the opportunity, but I believe I'll continue the search on my own."

"What will you do, next?"

215

"To be honest, I don't know, exactly."

"Would you like a suggestion?"

"Sure, why not?"

"We are the distribution point for freight that goes all over. The wagon drivers are in a position to know just about everything that goes on around here. Perhaps one of them will take you with them."

"Thanks. I might just try that."

Two privates were loading a wagon, while a man about Cade's age stood by, directing how he wanted the load to go. He was cleanshaven, except for a neatly trimmed moustache.

"Yes, Evans, that will do nicely," he said as one of the privates looked toward him before setting down the box. "That will help balance the load, and make it easier for the team to pull the wagon."

"Excuse me," Cade said.

"Yes, sir?" the wagon driver replied.

"My name is Cade McCall."

"Oh yes, you're the one trying to find his wife," the wagon driver replied.

"You know about that?"

"Mr. McCall, everyone on the post knows." The driver extended his hand. "I'm Jacob Harrison. What can I do for you?"

"General Sully suggested that it might be a good idea if I could ride with one of the wagon drivers. I'd try not to be a burden," Cade said. "And I can spell you at driving when you want a break, but best of all I have a strong back so I can help with the loading and unloading."

"That makes sense. I do run across quite a few people in diverse positions. That could be a rather significant base to gather leads."

Cade laughed.

"Have I said something you find amusing?"

"No, of course not. It's just that I've not run into many bullwhackers who have the command of the English language that you have."

"I didn't start out to be a freight wagon driver. After I graduated from university, I became an English professor at a men's college in Fulton, Missouri, but after a while, I got bored, so I moved west." Harrison smiled. "Actually, I find driving a wagon to be much more stimulating and, to be honest, considerably more lucrative than teaching."

"I understand what you're saying," Cade said. "But now, Professor, will you take me on as an assistant? Oh, and I'll work for free."

"Well, I was going to try to bargain with you about your pay, but I don't think I can do any better than 'free'. So yes, you're my new assistant."

Cade's association with Jacob Harrison was more productive than anything he had done before. His route took him north as far as Fort Hays, Kansas, south to Camp Supply in the Indian Territory, west as far as Fort Lyon, Colorado, and all towns, trading posts, and road ranches in between. He didn't get any information on where Arabella was, but as he spoke to traders and military, he began to narrow his search down to where she wasn't. He was convinced that she wasn't with Indians.

They had just crossed the Cimarron River and were in Indian Territory on their way to Fort Supply to deliver, among other things, a couple of cases of repeating rifles.

"I would like to have had a rifle like these we're delivering back when I was in the 33rd Tennessee," Cade said. "It sure would have come in handy."

"You know, I wasn't in the war," Jacob said. "But I was in the army, and I tried to get in on the fighting, but I never got out of St. Louis."

"Consider yourself lucky," Cade said. "I hate giving a Yankee general credit for anything, but Sherman was right when he said 'War is hell.' I can tell you for a fact that it really is."

"Well, here's another good thing about me not being in the war," Jacob said. "I was wearing blue, you were wearing gray."

"That I was, friend, that I was," Cade replied. "Say, if you don't mind, stop the wagon here, for a moment. I need to water the lilies."

"Good enough. I want to the check the harness anyway."

Cade was standing on the side of the road, relieving himself, when he saw something down in a gulley that caught his attention. As soon as he finished, he crawled down into the gulley to examine the object of his curiosity. It was a knife, with a wood handle, and a curved blade. The initials EH were carved into the handle. He had no idea how long it had been there, but it looked to be in pretty good condition, so he picked it up, planning to show it to Jacob. When he climbed back up to the top of the gulley, he saw Jacob sitting on the wagon seat with both hands raised. He also saw three men holding pistols on Jacob.

"We don't want your whole wagon," one of the men was saying. "All we want is them repeatin' rifles you're a' carryin'."

"What makes you think I have any repeating rifles?" Jacob asked.

"We know. Now, get shed o' them rifles 'n you can go on about your business."

"I've got an idea," Cade said, his words shocking the three road-agents who knew nothing about him. "Suppose we keep the rifles, and you three men just go on about your business?" Cade was holding a pistol.

"What the hell?" one of the men shouted and, swinging his gun toward Cade, he fired and missed.

Cade returned fire and didn't miss. The other two men turned toward Cade and guns roared. When the smoke cleared away, all three of the highwaymen were down, one of them shot by Jacob, who had taken advantage of the situation to get to his own gun.

"You all right, Jacob?" Cade called up to him.

"Yes, thanks to you. I'm quite sure they intended to leave no witnesses. We're in Indian Territory, so Indians would have been suspected."

Cade climbed back up into the wagon. "For a college professor, you're pretty handy with a gun."

"I've been around them for most of my life," Jacob replied. He chuckled. "But the saving factor here was your weak bladder. Had you not responded to a call of nature, you wouldn't have had the advantage over them. What were you doing down in the gulley, by the way? Surely, you aren't that modest."

"I found this," Cade said.

Jacob examined it for a moment. "A Solingen knife, used by buffalo skinners. And I know this one. It belongs to a grizzled old gentleman by the name of Ernst Hoffmann."

Three days later, they had delivered their cargo to Camp Supply in the Indian Territory, and were on their way back, when they stopped at the Buffalo Creek Trading Post. Cade was in the back of the store, looking at some woolen shirts, when Jacob came up to him.

"Are we ready to go?" Cade asked.

"No, not yet. There's somebody up here that I think you should meet."

"Oh?"

"It's Ernst Hoffmann."

Cade smiled. "He wants his knife back. Sure, I'll be glad to return it to him."

"It's more than that."

"What do you mean?"

"He may have some information you can . . . ."

Even before Jacob could finish his sentence, Cade was on the move.

". . . use," Jacob finished.

As Cade approached the front of the store he saw a big bear of a man, with white hair and a white beard.

"Mr. Hoffman?"

"*Jah*, I'm Hoffman."

"I believe this is your knife."

"*Jah. Danke,*" Hoffman said, taking the knife.

"Jacob, uh, that is, Mr. Harrison, said you might have some information I could use."

"You are looking for two women*, jah*?"

"Yes."

"I saw a buffalo hunter and skinner who had two women with them. I do not think the women were happy being with them."

"Where did you see them?"

"In Colorado, on Two Bit Creek. But I think they may not be the women you want to find."

"Why do you say that?"

"I do not think they are American women. They were in *Französisch sprechend?*"

"He said they were speaking in French," Jacob said with a big smile. He already knew all about Arabella and Magnolia.

"When?" Cade asked, excitedly. "When did you see them?"

"About a month, now."

"Jacob! That means they're still alive!"

"It sounds like it," Jacob said. "I think I'm about to lose my assistant."

"You knew all along I'd be leaving as soon as I heard something."

"I know," Jacob said. "But I'm going to miss you, Cade."

"Me too. When I get Arabella back, maybe she and I can meet up with you again."

"I have a suggestion for you if you want to take it."

"What's that?" Cade asked.

"Old Man Hoffman has a buffalo outfit, but his hunter left him. He's looking for a hunter."

"I can be that man, Mr. Hoffman," Cade said. "That is if you'll have me."

"You need big gun," Hoffman said.

"Big gun?"

"He means a Sharps fifty," the store keep said. "It'll bring down anything that walks on the face of this earth."

"I'll buy it," Cade said. "And as much fifty-caliber ammunition as you have available."

Cade proved to be a good hunter, and over the next few months he and Hoffman made a good team, with Cade killing the buffalo, and the German skinning them. Like Cade, Hoffman had also been in battle, fighting in two Prussian-Austrian wars, the first in 1864, and the second in 1866. He had come to America in 1867 declaring that if Prussia was going to fight a war every two years, he wanted no part of it.

It was now more than ten months since Arabella and Magnolia had disappeared, and six months since Cade had joined Hoffman. It was April, but the winter had hung on, and it was a cold, heavily overcast day. Cade had found a small herd of buffalo and had brought one down with his first shot. The herd moved on so he left the bull where it lay, and followed after them, sometimes riding, sometimes on foot. Then a heavy fog moved in, and looking around he realized that his horse was no longer in sight. The first approach of an icy cold norther whistled through the branches of the mesquite, and he called out to his horse, realizing that he needed to get out of the weather and back to the relative safety of the camp.

The horse didn't respond to his call. Darkness began to fall, which with the fog, made it impossible to see more than two or three feet in front of him. By now he had lost all sense of direction, and decided he should stop wandering around, for fear of getting even farther from the camp.

Then, in a stroke of luck, he happened across the body of one of the buffalo he had killed earlier, so he began skinning it. Soon he had the hide completely off the animal, and he wrapped up in it, hair-side in. The robe kept out the wind, and he was actually able to sleep.

He was awakened during the night by a pack of ravenous wolves that were devouring the carcass of the buffalo he had killed earlier. Then, to his horror he realized that they were also attacking the skin in which he was encased. The hide wrapped around him was meat-side out. Finally he was able to get to his pistol, and holding it up, shot one of the wolves. With a yelp, it fell to its side. The gunshot frightened the others away, but the wolves were drawn again and again to the feast, and during the night he killed three more, shooting them at point-blank range.

It began snowing, but stopped before morning and when dawn broke the sun was shining brightly, reflecting in a glare off the new-fallen snow. Throwing off the robe, he looked around for his horse, but didn't see it. When he found the other buffalos he had shot, he was able to get his bearings. He knew which way he needed to go to get back to camp, so he started walking through the snow. By mid-morning he saw Hoffman coming toward him in the wagon. He also saw his horse, tied to the back of the wagon.

"We will have coffee and breakfast now," Hoffman said as calmly as if this morning was no different from any other since they had come out.

The winter finally broke its hold, and the weather became mild. Cade was beginning to give up hope of ever finding Arabella again, though he never gave voice to such feelings, and even pushed the thought aside when it arose. In the meantime, anytime he and Hoffman ran into any other hunters or travelers, he asked the same question.

"Have you seen any buffalo hunters who have two white women with them?"

Then, in late May he got the answer he had been looking for.

"Yeah," someone said, "they's a couple of hunters I seen no more 'n two weeks ago that had two women 'n a baby with them."

"A baby?"

"Yeah, one of 'em's got herself a baby 'n it looks like the other'n's about to drop one. 'N I got the idea that Kilgore wasn't none too pleased about that."

"Kilgore?" Cade shouted the name. "Are you telling me that the man who has them is Amon Kilgore?"

"I didn' never hear his first name. But yeah, the two men was Kilgore 'n I think the other'n was callin' hisself Toombs. Didn' never learn the women's names though. They didn' neither one of 'em talk much, 'n when they did talk, they was talkin' in some language I couldn't understand."

"Where!" Cade asked. "Where did you see them?"

"It was down at Potato Butte."

Cade looked over at Hoffman.

"We could be there by tomorrow," Hoffman said.

26

The hunt ended suddenly, and unexpectedly, when they stopped at Dunnigan's Goods, a remote trading post on the Bent Canyon Road. While Hoffman was taking care of the team, Cade went inside.

"Hello, Mr. Dunnigan. We'll need some bacon, and flour."

"Cade?" a woman's voice asked, the words hesitant and somewhat apprehensive. "Cade is that you? Is it really you?"

Whirling toward the sound of the voice, Cade saw Magnolia, sitting on a sack of cornmeal as she nursed a baby.

"Maggie!" Cade shouted.

"We prayed for you to come for us," Magnolia said. "We prayed and we prayed, but finally we gave up hope." Tears were streaming down her cheeks.

"I'm here now," he said hurrying to her side. "Where's Arabella? Where is she?"

"She's here," Dunnigan said, his face somber.

"What's wrong?" Cade demanded. "Where's my wife?" He shouted the words.

"Take him to her," Magnolia said.

"Come with me. She's with my wife," Dunnigan said, leading Cade to the back of the store. He opened the door and when Cade looked in, he saw Arabella lying in bed, with a gray-haired woman putting a damp cloth to her forehead.

"Arabella!" he said, rushing to the side of the bed.

Arabella moved her hand toward Cade as a wan smile crossed her lips.

"My darling, Cade. You're here," Arabella said, her voice so weak that it could scarcely be heard. "But you're too late . . . too late." Her eyes closed.

"No, it's never too late," Cade said, lifting her hand to kiss it. "I love you, Arabella, I love you, and I've never stopped looking. Not from the day you disappeared."

"I'm glad I get to see you . . . one last time."

"What do you mean, one last time? I'm not going anywhere," Cade said, though he felt a sinking heart, because he could tell what she was saying by looking at her.

"Don't think that, Arabella. I've just found you and I'm not going to let you go."

"The baby," Arabella said. "I know it isn't yours but, please promise me, you'll not abandon the baby."

"We'll raise the baby together."

"No, I . . . I won't be with you."

"Of course you will," Cade insisted.

Arabella closed her eyes and grimaced as she reacted to a sudden, severe spasm of pain.

"Arabella!"

"The baby's coming," Mrs. Dunnigan said. "Get Magnolia in here."

Cade rushed back out into the store. "Maggie, the baby's coming! She needs you."

"Here," Maggie said, handing her baby to Cade. "Her name is Arabella."

Unsure of himself, Cade took the baby, holding it awkwardly, but securely. The store keep came over to him.

225

"You ain't never been around babies before, have you?" he asked.

"This is the first one I've ever held," Cade admitted.

"Hold her like this." Dunnigan adjusted the way Cade was holding the baby so both were more comfortable.

"How long ago did Kilgore drop Arabella and Maggie off here?"

"What do you mean?"

"I expect Maggie with a baby, and Arabella pregnant, he didn't have any use for them anymore, so that's why he left them here."

"Mister, this feller Kilgore you're talkin' about, he didn't leave 'em here. He left 'em out in the middle of nowhere, with no food, no water, nothin'."

"Then I don't understand. How did they get here?"

"An old Arapaho injun by the name of Nartana found 'em. Him 'n his squaw brung 'em in yesterday mornin' on a couple of travois. It was a good thing they did, too, 'cause it ain't likely none of 'em would 'a lived more 'n another couple of days. 'Specially the baby. Her mama had near 'bout run out of milk."

"You mean the bastards just left them to die?"

"Yes, sir, near as I can figure, that's exactly what I mean."

"Cade!" Maggie called, though it could better be described as a scream. "Come quick!"

"I'll take the young'un. You go," Dunnigan said.

Cade ran into the back room and the first thing he saw was the massive amount of blood in the bed.

"Arabella!" he screamed. "No, no, not now. I've just found you, you can't go."

He knelt by her bed, and she turned toward him, her hand reaching out to touch his face. She rubbed her finger over his lips. "The baby, is it a boy, or a girl?"

Cade looked toward Mrs. Dunnigan. "It's a girl," she said.

"You have . . ." Cade started, then he corrected himself. "*We* have a beautiful little girl. She looks just like you. Lots of dark hair. She's beautiful."

"What do you want to name her?"

"I know. I want to name her the most beautiful name I know, Chantal." He moved over Arabella to kiss her. "If it wouldn't have been for Chantal, I would never have met the most wonderful woman in the world."

"Promise me you'll take care of her. Chantal. I like that."

"I told you . . . *we* will take care of . . ."

"I won't be here. You'll have to . . ."

Arabella took a couple of gasping breaths, then she stopped breathing. Cade watched the life leave her eyes.

"No!" he shouted. He buried his head onto the side of the bed and held her hand as hard as he could. "No!" he cried again, as the tears began to flow.

Magnolia knelt beside Cade, then pulled his head into her bosom, as they wept together.

"Sie ist mit Gott, Cade. Sie ist mit Gott," Hoffman said reverently. Both he and Dunnigan, still holding Magnolia's baby, had come into the room, and were standing, quietly.

Three months later:

Cade stood in the anteroom of the Fort Dodge Chapel, waiting with Jeter.

"I can't believe she said she would marry me," Jeter said. "I never thought I would get married. I'm the luckiest man in the world."

"Magnolia is a wonderful woman, Jeter. I agree, you are a lucky man. And if you won't get the big head with me saying so, you're a good man, too, willing to take on an entire family."

"I intend to raise Chantal and Arabella just as if they were sisters," Jeter promised.

"I promised that I wouldn't abandon Chantal, and I won't," Cade said. "But she'll have to stay with Magnolia as long as she's nursing."

Jeter smiled. "You're calling her Magnolia now."

"Yes, because that's what Arabella called her."

Jeter stepped to the door and looked out into the nave of the chapel. "Ma's wearin' the biggest grin you ever saw," he said, speaking of Mary Hatley who was sitting in the very first row.

"She didn't mind us selling the MW?"

"Not when I told her I was movin' to Buffalo City. She said there was no way she intended to stay there."

The chaplain opened the door to the anteroom. "Mr. Willis, it's time for you to meet your bride," he said, with a big smile.

After the wedding, Jeter and Cade built The Red House, a saloon in the town of Buffalo City, which some were already calling Dodge City. Cade was a silent partner in The Red House, silent because he had nothing to do with its day to day operation. Cade had signed on with the same freighting company as Jacob Harrison, using the mobility of the wagon travel as a way to search for Kilgore and Toombs.

It was six months after the wedding, and he was at the Lee and Reynolds Trading Station on the Cimarron down in Indian Territory, when Ron Lee stepped out to the wagon to speak to him.

"Cade, are you still looking for Kilgore and Toombs?"

"Yes."

"I heard they have a shack over on King Fisher Creek. That's about ten miles west of here."

"Are you sure that's them?"

"I'm sure. They're making a lot of money, selling whiskey to the Indians."

"And nobody stops them?"

"They're paying off the Indian police, and nobody else goes that way."

"Thanks, Ron, if you don't mind, I'm going to leave the team and wagon with you for a few days. Do you have a horse and saddle I might use."

Lee nodded. "I figured you'd want to go find 'em."

King Fisher Creek:

Kilgore walked out of the shack with an Indian who was clutching a bottle of whiskey.

"You tell your friends that there's a lot more where this came from," Kilgore said.

"You charge too much for whiskey," the Indian said.

Kilgore laughed. "Well, you can always go somewhere else to get it," he said. "Oh, wait, there isn't any place else you can get it, is there?"

As the Indian hopped onto his pony, and rode away, Toombs came over to stand beside Kilgore.

"We're goin' to have to get some more whiskey, pretty soon."

"Ahh, we got ten full bottles 'n ten empty bottles," Kilgore said. "We can stretch that into twenty full bottles with a little water."

"We already done that with the full bottles we got," Toombs said.

"They're a bunch o' ignert savages. They ain't never goin' to know the difference," Kilgore insisted.

"You know what I miss?" Toombs asked.

"What's that?"

Toombs grabbed his crotch and flashed a leering smile. "I miss havin' them two women around anytime we wanted 'em."

"Yeah, well, when they started sproutin' babies, they was more trouble 'n they was worth," Kilgore said.

"We could'a killed the babies just like a tomcat does," Toombs said. "What'a you reckon happened to 'em? I mean, when we went back they warn't there no more."

"I expect the wolves et 'em," Kilgore said.

"Maybe we could get us a couple o' injun squaws 'n . . ." that was as far as Toombs got, before the side of his head burst open with blood, brain, and bone detritus spewing forth.

Kilgore stood for a long moment, so shocked by what he had just seen that he didn't have time to be afraid. He never knew when the second .50 caliber bullet smashed into his head, dropping his body on top of Toombs.

Five hundred yards away, Cade rose from the prone position, slipped the Sharps Buffalo rifle back into the saddle sheath, and returned to the Lee and Reynold's Trading Post. He needed to get the wagon back to Fort Dodge.

Epilogue

Twin Creek Ranch, Howard County, Texas – 1927:

"I know, I know," Cade said, "you're wondering why I didn't face them down, instead of shooting them from more than a quarter mile away. Well, I thought about it, and there's no doubt in my mind that I could have taken both of them fairly easily."

"Then why didn't you?" Owen Wister asked. "I mean, it seems to me like you would have had more personal satisfaction from letting them know that you caught up with them, and that they were paying for their misdeeds."

Cade shook his head. "They're just as dead. During the war I killed a lot of men who never saw the shot coming, and I killed them only because they were on the other side, and that was the nature of war. If good men could be killed in such a way, I felt no compunction about killing Kilgore and Toombs like that."

"Were there ever any repercussions from you shooting them?" Owen Wister asked.

"No. I told Lee that I couldn't find them. The only people I ever told were Jacob Harrison and Jeter, and, of course, Magnolia. I felt like she should know."

"How did she take it?"

Cade smiled. "She kissed me. Right in front of Jeter, she kissed me. Then she explained, to both of us, that the kiss was from Arabella."

"You still miss Arabella, don't you? After all these years."

"Yeah, Dan, I miss her, just as I know Molly misses Jacob. I think one of the things that has strengthened our marriage over the years, more than half a century now, is that we've been able to share our love with Jacob and Arabella."

"Speaking of Arabella, and Chantal, too. Where are they, today?"

"I'm really proud of Chantal. She's the head mistress of Irvinson Girls' School in Laramie, Wyoming. Of course, since she went into teaching, she never got married, but she says the school girls are her family."

"And Arabella?"

"She's a grandmother in Ft. Worth, and Magnolia lives with her now that Jeter has passed."

From out front, they heard a car horn honking.

Amanda stuck her head into the library.

"Grandpa, Mr. Wister, my boyfriend is here. He wants to drive us all into Big Spring for dinner. I told him I could talk you into it. Will you please come with us?"

"Wait a minute, Amanda, are you telling me you want two old geezers like Dan and me to come along on your date?"

"You're not old, Grandpa," Amanda said as she grabbed his hand. "And yes, I want you to come.

"All right," Cade said, with a chuckle. "But promise me there won't be any spooning or anything."

"Grandpa, don't say that," Amanda said as she helped to pull him to his feet. "So, tell me, Mr. Wister, did grandpa tell you everything?"

"No, darlin'," Wister replied. "I have a feeling this saga is just getting started."

About the Author

Robert Vaughan sold his first book when he was 19. That was 57 years and nearly 500 books ago. He wrote the novelization for the mini series *Andersonville*. Vaughan wrote, produced, and appeared in the History Channel documentary Vietnam Homecoming. His books have hit the NYT bestseller list seven times. He has won the Spur Award, the PORGIE Award (Best Paperback Original), the Western Fictioneers Lifetime Achievement Award, received the Readwest President's Award for Excellence in Western Fiction, is a member of the American Writers Hall of Fame and is a Pulitzer Prize nominee. Vaughn is also a retired army officer, helicopter pilot with three tours in Vietnam. And received the Distinguished Flying Cross, the Purple Heart, The Bronze Star with three oak leaf clusters, the Air Medal for valor with 35 oak leaf clusters, the Army Commendation Medal, the Meritorious Service Medal, and the Vietnamese Cross of Gallantry.

Find more great titles by Robert Vaughan and Wolfpack Publishing at http://wolfpackpublishing.com/robert-vaughan/

Made in the USA
Middletown, DE
11 July 2022

69028100R00137